falling for DR. KELLY

When opposites attract, it's explosive

A Falling novel
by DL Gallie

**Every force has an equal and opposite attraction.
Love being the most volatile of them all.**

AVERY

My life is anything but boring.
So what if I'm an introvert and prefer to focus on my career?
I was fine.
Until I met him—Flynn Kelly.
The doctor with the sexy Irish accent.
I thought we were unbreakable, until someone close hurts me in an unimaginable way.
Can two opposites fight the laws of attraction or will it end up tearing us apart?

FLYNN

I work hard, and play even harder.
When it came to women, I could have anyone I want.
Until I met her—Avery Evans.
She's quiet, shy, and everything I'm not.
But we're drawn together like magnets, sparking each other to life.
When the unthinkable happens, our differences really show.
Is our attraction about to sizzle and flame out? Only time will tell.

ALSO BY DL GALLIE

STAND ALONES

Out of Nowhere

Antecedent

Seven Nights

Falling for Dr. Kelly, a Falling novel

Falling for Dr. Knight, a Falling novel

Falling for Agent Cox, a Falling novel - COMING LATE 2020

The Rule Breaker anthology

Doc Steel

In the Dark of Night anthology

THE CASTAWAY GROVE COLLECTION

Love has arrived in the Grove

Oasis

Unequivocal Love

Five Words

…and a few more to come.

THE LIQUOR CABINET SERIES

Liquor has never been so disturbingly saucy

Malt Me (Book 1)

Tequila Healing (Book 2)

Wine Not (Book 3)

The Final Shot (Book 4)

The Liquor Cabinet: Series boxset

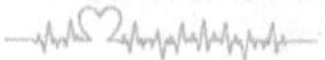

THE UNEXPECTED SERIES

When it comes to love, expect the unexpected

The Unexpected Gift

The Unexpected Letter

The Unexpected Package

The Unexpected Connection

To Halle,
Dr. Kelly is all yours

"You know you're in love when you can't fall asleep because reality is finally better than your dreams."

~ Dr Seuss

PROLOGUE

BAYLOR AND I ARE LYING UNDER HER BED GIGGLING LIKE schoolgirls. "That was awesome, BayBay. They had no idea it was me."

"I know, Avie, I know." Bay says with a smile that lights up her face. "We should do this again. It's so much fun playing each other."

"It sure is." I look to my twin sister and smile, happy that of all the people in the world I ended up with her as my twin. She's my BayBay.

"I love that you're my sister, Avie."

"And I love that you're mine too, BayBay. We are gonna be twinsies forever."

"What's a twinsie?" she asks.

"It's your twin, who is also your best friend," I explain to my older twin, by seven minutes.

"Twinsies forever," she whispers back. "Let's do it again and this time let's do it for a whole day."

"Yes, let's do it tomorrow."

As the memory fades and reality kicks back in, a sadness washes over me. Baylor and I were close and we swore we'd be twinsies forever, and up until recently, we were. She was one of my best friends, albeit selfish at times, but at the end of the day, she always had my back and I had hers. We were there for one another when we needed a shoulder to cry on or a hug just because. But she's changing before my eyes and turning into a horrible, despicable person. My BayBay, my twinsie, is wilting away and there's nothing I can do about it. This new Baylor is harsh and not a nice person to be around. She's always been the headstrong, outgoing, and brash twin, the complete opposite to me. I'm shy, quiet, and reserved. Some would say I'm a pushover but differences aside, we always had each other's back.

I want that Baylor back.

My BayBay.

I don't like this new one.

Today is my last day at Oasis, what I thought was going to be a sex-filled getaway didn't quite turn out how I expected. The first few days I hooked up each night but they were nothing to write home about, and then I met Paige Walsh. Paige is a smoking hot red-haired vixen and, rather than getting down and dirty between the sheets with her, we became friends. Platonic, no hanky-panky, non-kissing friends…and then she got back together with her fiancé and I really was relegated to the friend zone. If I'm honest, I'm glad Paige got her happily ever after, she deserves more than a weekend fuckfest with me. My dick, on the other hand, he isn't too happy with me right now. The term blue balls is an accurate description of my nether regions at this moment in time.

I just bumped into Paige and Cam, her douche fiancé—he broke her heart and then game grovelling back, hence douche fiancé reference—but Paige is beaming right now. From the chats we had, he is the rum to her Coke and when he followed her here, it cemented her feelings for him. *Lucky bastard.* After walking away from them, I head down to the beach for one last swim before my flight home. Kicking off my flip-flops, I pull my shirt over my head, and drop my sunglasses on top of my shirt. Looking around, I see I'm the only one here, so I pull down my boardshorts and I run toward the ocean, naked as the day I was born. When the water is to my knees, I dive in, the water is cold and a shock to the system, but it's just what I need.

Breaking the surface, I shake my head from side to side, flicking water droplets around like a dog. Floating on my back, I stare up at the sky, it's the bluest of blue and there's not a cloud in sight. I'll be sad to leave this place, but after losing Paige—not that I had her in the first place—I think getting back to Chicago is what the doctor—me—ordered.

I really needed this getaway, the last few weeks at the hospital have been crazy busy. So busy I haven't even had a chance to hook up in the on-call room. It used to be great when Kristin Payne worked there. She and I had a mutual arrangement that worked for both of us. The sex was mind-blowing, there were no feelings or awkwardness; it worked great between us. Until she foolishly went and fell in love with her childhood best friend. But in saying that, I've never seen her happier. It was no surprise when she ended our arrangement. Was I sad? Sure, but I was happy she was happy. A few weeks later, he took a job in

Australia and she left with him. Leaving me and my blue balls behind.

I've had enough with the moping, so I stand up and dive back under the water. When I break the surface, I swim until my arms hurt. I'm a fair way out from shore and if I'm honest, I'm impressed with how far I swam. Looking at my watch, I see I have to get back; otherwise I'll miss my flight. Swimming back to shore, I slip my shorts back on, grab the rest of my stuff, and head to my room where I shower and change for the flight home. While I'm in the shower, like I have the last few days, I pleasure myself to thoughts of Paige, wishing ever so hard it really were her. Closing my eyes, I imagine it's her hand gripping my cock and pumping. Squeezing the tip before sliding her palm down my shaft. My balls tighten and I come over the shower wall, murmuring her name as I empty my load.

Opening my eyes, I step under the showerhead, letting the droplets cascade over my shoulders, washing away the remnants of my self-love. Soaping up, I clean myself, climb out, dry off, and finish packing.

After checking out, I jump on the shuttle bus and it takes me to the airport, where I board my flight and head back to reality.

Preston Knight, my best friend and the best pediatric doctor at Western General, picks me up. "How was paradise?"

"Paradise," I forlornly reply.

"Why so glum?" I sigh, not sure what to say to him. "Dude, like seriously, what's up?"

"I have blue balls."

Preston laughs, a deep belly laugh which echoes through the car. I'm glad we are stopped at a red light;

otherwise, I'm sure he would have crashed the car. "Are you telling me, Dr. 'I have an accent, drop your panties now' has blue balls?"

Nodding my head, I sigh dejectedly, "Yep."

"How? You just got back from a fuckin' adults-only haven."

"The first few days were banging—pun intended—and then I met this chick but she was…"

"Was what?" he questions, as he pulls onto the freeway.

"She was there after a breakup—"

"Rebound sex," he interrupts, raising his eyebrows suggestively.

"I wish. The ex-fiancé arrived. He followed her to Oasis and won her back." *Lucky bastard.*

"Well shit, so why not hook up with someone else?"

"I don't know. I just wasn't feeling it. After getting cockblocked by her, I just, I don't know. If I'm honest, this weirdness goes further back. Ever since Kristin fell in love and moved to kangaroo land, I've just been out of sorts."

"Sounds like you need to get laid and you need to get laid good."

"Tell me about it. The boys are turning blue and I'm getting callouses on my hands from all the jacking off. I feel like a teenager again."

"If you like, we can go out tonight."

Shaking my head, I resist, "Nah, I need to get home, unpack, and get my head back into the game. Plus, I've got an early shift tomorrow."

"No worries, some other time then."

The rest of the trip to my place is silent. We pull up to my building and I climb out. Preston hops out and opens the trunk. Leaning in, I grab my bag. "Thanks for picking me up, man…and the talk."

"Anytime, you know that."

"Appreciate it. I'll see you tomorrow." Turning around, I head inside. The doorman, *he's new*, I think to myself, opens the door and nods at me. Nodding at the desk clerk, I push the button for the penthouse. The elevator arrives, I step in and the car whisks me up to my floor.

Stepping into my penthouse, I look around. It really is a bachelor pad, but it's MY bachelor pad. Everything is dark brown. My couch, the rug, the artwork. Hell, even the kitchen has chocolate brown granite and dark wooden cabinets. At least the walls are light, brightening the place up. As I head into my bedroom, I think maybe it's time to overhaul this place. If I lighten the furnishings up, it might lighten my mood as well.

Dropping my suitcase off in the walk-in closet, I head back to the kitchen and pour myself a glass of red. I'm thankful I called my housekeeper and asked her to stock up today. Not wanting a heavy meal, I prepare a cheese platter and head out to the patio. I enjoy my wine and watch the sun go down. The sensor lights flick on and I realize I've been sitting out here for hours.

Picking up the empty plate and my wine, I head inside. Placing the plate and glass in the sink, I head to bed, hoping a goodnight's sleep will reset my mood, and I'll be ready to head back to work in the morning. I drift off to sleep and for the first night since meeting Paige, I don't dream of her. I take it as a good sign and that things will return to normal.

AVERY

"For fuck's sake, Bay," I growl, as I walk into the kitchen. It's already been a long day since I had parent-teacher conferences today, and then after I left school, I had to stop in at Jewel-Osco to get a few things. Placing the grocery bags on the floor in the kitchen, I look around at the mess Baylor left and shake my head. What has gotten into my sister lately? It looks like she cooked up a greasy breakfast, using every dish we own, and then left everything where it was. She even left the butter and milk on the counter. Grabbing them, I place them away in the refrigerator and grab the two bottles of wine—hey, it was two-for-one—and the other cold grocery items while I'm at it.

Grabbing my phone, I connect it to the Bose system and I groove out to The Killers, singing along to "Mr. Brightside" as I put the other food in the pantry. Turning from the pantry, I look to the sink. "Fuck me," I groan, the sink is full of dirty dishes, actually it's overflowing with greasy, grimy dishes. I shudder at the sight before me. Bay has always been the messy twin, but this is absolutely disgusting. The counter next to the sink is also covered with dirty dishes and cups. I'm embarrassed to be related to the slob who created this mess. Opening the dishwasher, I get a reprieve when I see it's empty. I get to work loading the dishwasher with as many of the dishes as possible. And surprisingly, I get most of them in, which was more than I anticipated. Once it's full, I pop in a tablet and turn it on.

Then I tackle what's left.

Filling the sink with hot water, I wash and scrub for what feels like hours. Once they are all sparkly and clean, I pop them in the drying rack, no way am I drying them up too. Then I turn my attention to the pots and pans that were left on the stove. Emptying the sink, for the third time, I clean the pots and pans and then put them on the stovetop to dry, since the rack is full but first, I need to remove the grease and food splatters from the stove. With the dishes and stove taken care of, I start on the countertops and cupboards because something is splattered on them. Note to self, when I move again, do not get a kitchen with white cabinets. This job takes me just as long as it did to wash the pots. The grease had started to set but with a little elbow grease—pun intended—the kitchen is finally spotless.

With a sigh, I throw the cloth into the trash, no saving

that one. Leaning against the cabinets, I look around and smile. I really love our place, Bay and I made it into a real home. It suits both our personalities. The kitchen is small, with white upper and lower cabinets. The countertops are a speckled gray with a coffee maker and toaster sitting out for easy access. The kitchen is off the dining nook, which has a round table with four chairs. Off there is the living room, which consists of our sofa, coffee table, entertainment unit with flat-screen TV, stereo, and DVD player. It opens to a reasonably sized balcony, which overlooks the park across the road. The balcony is large enough for two chairs, a lounger, and small table. At the back of the living room is the front door and hallway, which leads to the two bedrooms and a half bath. There are faux wooden floorboards throughout and plush carpets in the bedroom. The bonus of this place, each room has its own en suite so I don't need to share with Bay. She never used to be this much of a slob but lately, her habits have been slipping.

Opening the fridge, I pull out my bottle of wine and pour myself a glass, a well-deserved glass after playing Suzy Homemaker since I got home. Taking a sip, I close my eyes and savor the taste as the pinot grigio slides down my throat. Not in the mood to cook, I put together a mini platter, consisting of smoked cheese, salami, olives, and crackers. With my platter and wine in hand, I walk into the living room and my heart sinks. This room is just as messy. Not wanting to deal with it right now, I step out onto the balcony, which is surprisingly tidy.

Climbing onto the lounger, I place the platter next to me and lie back. Finally I'm able to relax. For the rest of the evening, I enjoy my wine and food. Bay doesn't come home and she doesn't call either, her behavior is concerning at the moment. However, as Cress keeps telling me, Bay is old enough to look after herself, but I worry about my twin. There's a niggling feeling deep inside my stomach, telling me she's in trouble, and I don't like feeling like this. I really hope I'm just being a worrywart right now.

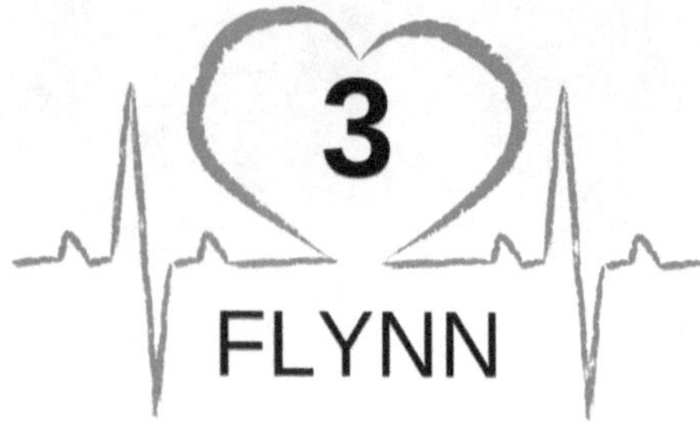

FLYNN

"Time of death: five fifty-two," I declare, shaking my head in defeat. Someone pats my back in sympathy, and I let out a deep sigh. It's tough losing a patient. It doesn't matter if they are ninety or nine, a life is a life. Now the sucky part, I have to face the family and let them know that we, I, was unable to save their dad/brother/husband/son. This is the part that hurts the most. Sure, losing a patient stinks, but seeing those left behind fall apart, that's heartbreaking and it never gets easier. Thankfully, it doesn't happen all the time, but when it does, it messes with me and I doubt everything I did as the doctor on the case. Was there something I could have done to prevent the death? Did I fuck up? Doubt is a bitch, especially in my line of work.

Running my hands though my hair, I take a deep breath to prepare myself; not that you can really prepare for this. Exiting the room, I wash my hands and make my way out to the waiting room. As soon as I step into the waiting room, a lady stands up. She looks at me and without me even uttering a word, she knows. Her face pales. She begins to shake her head from side to side and lifts her hand to cover her mouth. The first tear falls as I begin walking toward her. "Mrs. Hunter" She nods but doesn't utter a word, "I'm Dr. Kelly. I was working on your husband, Paul. Unfortunately, due to the injuries he sustained in the crash, I was unable to save him." *To the point. Direct, without being harsh.* They are the words my mentor told me the first time I lost a patient and to this day, I still repeat them to myself when I deliver news like this.

"No. No. No!" she wails. She falls forward and crashes into me. She rests her palms and forehead on my chest, shaking her head from side to side repeating "No" over and over.

It isn't until a little voice says, "Mommy," that I realize he was a father. Mrs. Hunter really loses it when she looks down at her daughter. She drops down to her knees and envelops the little girl in her arms and cries harder. Seeing this causes a lump to form in the back of my throat when it really hits me: I didn't save this little girl's dad. *Fuck, fuck, fuck.*

Lifting my hand, I squeeze the back of my neck and look down at this woman and her daughter. My heart breaks for them both, it aches in a way I've never felt before. Reaching out, I rub Mrs. Hunter's back as she continues to cry, holding her little girl tightly to her chest.

She's sobbing uncontrollably but at the same time, whispering to her daughter.

The little girl pulls away from her mom and looks up at me; her eyes red and filled with tears. "Why didn't you save my daddy?"

Wow, this little girl just gutted it me further with her words. I didn't think I could feel any shittier than I already do but this lil' one just knocked me on my ass once again. Dropping to my knees, I look her in the eyes. "I'm sorry sweetheart, I did everything I could to save your daddy."

She looks over to her mother, her bottom lip quivering and the tears in her eyes spilling down her little cheeks. "Daddy's not coming home," she tearfully cries.

"No, honey, he's not," Mrs. Hunter replies softly.

Reaching out, I take her hand and squeeze. "I know it'll be hard to never see or hug your daddy again, but he's in heaven now. You've now got your very own angel. He will look over you, protect you, and love you forever and ever."

The little girl looks to her mom. "Is that true, Mommy? Is Daddy an angel now?"

"Yes, honey, he is." She swallows a sob, "And what do angels do?"

"Angels ALWAYS smile down on those they care about."

"That's right."

"But if he loves us, why did he leave us?" *Wow, can this child gut me anymore?*

Her mother gasps and begins to sob. She drops to her knees and envelops her daughter in her arms, and together they cry and grieve. I give them a few moments and then reach out and squeeze her shoulder. "Sorry, Mrs. Hunter, but I need to talk to you about organ dona—"

"Yes." Her head pops up and she looks directly into my eyes. "Yes, P-p-p-p…Paul wanted to. The least we can do is make his death worthwhile."

This woman is amazing. She has just lost her husband, the father of her child, and she's turning his death into something wonderful. People continue to surprise me, and for once, it's in a great way. Nodding my head, I squeeze her shoulder tighter. "I'll contact the team and someone will be over to see you shortly to sign some forms." She nods at me as the tears continue to streak down her cheeks. With a sad smile, I once again say, "I'm so sorry for your loss, Mrs. Hunter."

She continues to nod and cry as I walk away. Just as I reach the security doors, I hear a little scream echo through the room. Looking back, I see the little girl in her mother's arms, sobbing her little heart out. Now that's heartbreaking. Leaving the little girl and her mother to grieve, I push through the doors and make a beeline for the drug room. Slipping inside, I close the door and lean my head against the wall. Closing my eyes, I breathe deeply and sigh. Quietly I whisper, "Six words have never cut me so deeply before. That little girl's life will forever be changed because I couldn't save her father."

Turning around, I slide down the wall and rest my head back. Closing my eyes again, I breathe deeply and take a few moments to compose myself. The life of a doctor is shit some days, and today it is epically shit.

Once I feel like me again, well as much as you can after an incident like this, I stand up, shake it off, and head back to work. Pushing open the door, I swallow down the lump in my throat and get back to work.

Along the way, I pass a nurse and she looks seductively at me. Licking her lips and grinning. My eyes drop to her mouth and I remember those lips wrapped about my cock a few weeks ago in the on-call room. Then I look into her eyes and I recall the days after. If it hadn't have been for Kristin saving my ass, I would have had a stage five clinger on my hands. I think she's the reason for not hooking up with anyone after Kristin left. Nodding at her, I put my head down and keep walking. *Not today, nurse, not today…or ever again.*

Once everything is finalized, and I've handed things over to the transplant team, I pop the paperwork in the correct tray for filing and head toward the doctors' lounge, thankful today is finally over. Pushing the door open, I step in and see Miranda and Grant, sitting very close together; seems there's a hot new couple at Western General. I'm happy for them, but coupledom isn't for me. I'm made for giving pleasure, not settling. We nod our heads hello as I pass by. Sitting in front of my locker, I sigh when I hear the door open and close again.

"Dude," Preston says, I look up and see him walking over to me. Standing up, we do the manly slap on the back, one-armed man hug, and then I sit back down. "Sorry about your patient," he offers, as he opens his locker and begins to change; the dude has no shame whatsoever.

"Thanks, man. How he held on as long as he did is beyond me. There was literally nothing I could've done."

"That's tough."

Nodding, I pull my scrub top over my head, leaving me in a white T-shirt; I throw my top at the laundry cart and lean into my locker for my button-down. Holding the shirt in my hands, I rub my forehead, and turn to Preston. "Drinks?"

"Hell yes. It's been a tough week."

"It sure has. Doesn't even feel like I had a vacation, but I'm glad to have the weekend off, especially after today." As I say this, I think back to my holiday and the babes I hooked up with, and in particular the lass who got away, Paige Walsh. Just thinking about her has my cock twitching. Even now, a week later, I'm still thinking about the chick I didn't fuck. She's all I can think about. A night with a random lass is exactly what I need to get her out of my head, and I need someone who doesn't work here. That's a complication I don't need right now.

Thirty minutes later, Preston and I walk into the Fat Fox Tavern. We decided to skip the bar closest to Western General. After today, I didn't want to be around other doctors where the topic of conversation always turns to work. After what transpired with the death of Mr. Hunter, I do not want to think about being a doctor. Tonight I want to fuck and forget.

Glancing around the bar, my eyes land on the most beautiful woman I have ever seen. Chocolate brown hair cascades down her back. Slim waist, from what I can tell. Legs that go on and on, *I'd like to see those sexy as hell legs wrapped around my waist...or face.* She's sitting at the bar with a girlfriend, drinking beer and doing shots. *She's doesn't look like a prissy stuck-up lass*, I think to myself, as I watch her throw back a shot. She makes a face, which on anyone else would look silly, but on her, it's sexy as fuck. She downs another shot straight after garnering a laugh from her friend. This time she shakes her head at the hit of alcohol, and it causes her tits to wobble. From where I'm standing near the door, they look like gorgeous breasts. *I wanna bury my face in them, maybe even slide my dick between them.* At that thought, my dick twitches in my pants.

Discreetly adjusting myself, Preston and I walk farther

into the Tavern. We end up at the opposite end of the bar, which luckily for me, gives me a clear view of this sexy as hell vixen. We order two Guinnesses and head to a table in the back where again, I have a clear line of sight to the gorgeous brown-haired goddess who I cannot take my eyes off.

As I drink my beer, I hope and pray that later this evening, she will be riding my cock into the wee hours of the morning.

4

AVERY

My best friend Cressida (Cress) Bayliss and I have just arrived at The Fat Fox Tavern. Taking a seat at the bar, we order a round of beers and some shots. While we wait, Cress looks around the bar, no doubt scouting for tonight's hookup since she's child-free for the evening. Cress is a single mom to Lexi, and her daughter is a mini version of her mother. She's an exact carbon copy, looks and personality-wise. Good luck to Cress when Lexi is a teenager.

Our drinks are placed in front of us. We pick up our beers and tap them together and chant, "Cheers" before taking a sip. The yeasty goodness instantly relaxes me and I smile. Closing my eyes, I let the anguish of Baylor and the busy week I've had float away and vanish.

We sink our shots and I shake my head as the alcohol both burns and warms my body from the inside out. Picking up my beer, I take another drink when the sound of Cress's voice brings me back into the present. "Ave, there's a hottie Mc-fuckin'-Hotterson behind you and he is currently eye fucking the hell out of you from across the bar," Cress says, as she lifts her beer to her lips. Moving my shoulder, I go to turn and look but she grabs my arm roughly and whisper-shouts, "No! Don't look."

My eyes bug open. "Why? If he's so hot, I wanna see," I complain. I can tell from the look in her eyes that he is a twenty out of ten.

Her eyes bug wide open and then she starts to grin, leaving me antsy—a grinning Cress can be dangerous at times. Her eyes are steadfastly locked behind me. He really must be hot if she can't stop staring. And then it hits me, he's staring at her and not me, and she clearly wants him too. *Ohh well,* I think to myself as I pick up my beer and take another sip.

When her mouth drops open, I become confused. She's stunned silent. With her eyes bulged wide open and her mouth wide open. And then I feel it, a warmth at my back.

My skin prickles.

My heart rate accelerates.

My mouth goes dry.

The air around me crackles.

I've never had a reaction like this before…and I haven't even laid eyes on this guy. Closing my eyes, I inhale deeply and spin my chair, trying to look sexy as I do, but instead, I overexert and the stool flies around faster than I anticipated and I lose my balance. Reaching my hand out to brace myself on the edge of the bar I miss, and instead, my hand lands on a body, with a thump, in the most inappropriate of spots. A grunt emanates from above me and he doubles over. "Fuck me," he groans in pain.

"Holy shitballs, I'm so so sorry. Are you okay?"

"I will be…eventually," he groans through clenched teeth, "but would you mind removing you hand from my junk?"

I'm frozen.

I'm shocked.

I'm in awe of his voice.

His looks.

His accent.

And I'm red with embarrassment.

My eyes bore into the Adonis before me. Finally my brain kicks into gear and I realize my hand is still resting on his junk. "Oh my God. Shit. Sorry," I stammer, as I remove my hand from his impressive package. I quickly pull it back and my eyes wander over his body. Oh My Fucking God, this man is gorgeous. Drop-fucking-dead-gorgeous. Brown cropped hair. Blue eyes I could stare at for hours and lose myself in. Chiselled chin, covered in the right amount of scruff. And a dimple, a fucking dimple. "I'm so sorry. Are you okay?"

"Yeah, nothing an ice pack and a beer won't fix."

"Well, I can help you with the beer," I offer.

He stares at me and nods. "Aye, I'd like that." *Holy shit, his accent is hot, so fucking hot.*

His electric blue eyes stare intently at me. My skin heats from the intensity of his gaze. I'm sure my chest is bright red and blotching with my nervous rash, or just red with embarrassment, or a little of both. My hazel eyes stare back at him and I feel a connection with him, which is weird considering I just met him.

The moment is broken when the bartender says, "What

can I get for you?"

My eyes snap toward him. "Beer," I say, as I turn back to the man beside me. "A..."

"Guinness," he orders, his Irish accent again sending shivers through my body.

He offers me his hand. "Flynn, Flynn Kelly."

"Avery Evans," I reply. "Nice to meet you, Mr. Kelly."

"Doctor," he huskily replies.

"My mistake." I swallow and add, "It's nice to meet you, Dr. Flynn Kelly." Placing my hand in his, an electrical current zaps between us. It's just like those romantic moments I read about in my romance books.

"Tis a pleasure to meet you too, Avery Evans." My name sounds so sexy come from his lips, my eyes drop to his mouth, and I watch as his tongue darts out, sliding across his bottom lip.

We each hold each other's hand longer than appropriate and once again the barman interrupts us, delivering Flynn his beer. *Fucking cockblocker*, I think to myself, as I hand over a ten dollar bill to cover his drink.

"Thanks for the beer, Avery Evans." The way he says my name sets my body alight. Combine that with the intensity of his gaze and my body is a burning inferno. I love hearing his accented, deep husky voice wrap around each vowel and consonant within my name; hell, he could read the phone book to me and I'd be mesmerized. He takes a sip of beer, and my eyes watch as he swallows, it's sexy as all fuck. Yes, him drinking a beer is sexy. He places the beer on the bar top, his gaze once again boring into me. My body temperate is nearing catastrophic heat levels.

"My pleasure," I quietly offer in reply, brushing my hair over my shoulder as I stare at the gorgeous Irishman before me.

"It can be," he seductively says; as he continues to unabashedly fuck me with his eyes...again. My panties dampen. My tongue darts out and I lick my bottom lip. His eyes trace my tongue before I can register what's happening. He threads his fingers into my hair, pulls me toward him, and slams his lips against mine. My mouth opens in shock and he takes the opportunity to slide his tongue inside. My eyes close and I lose myself to the kiss. Our tongues seductively slide against one another. Our lips press together tightly. This kiss is not suitable for public, but I can't stop kissing him. My lips and tongue are moving on their own, I have no control. Sliding my hands into his hair, I pull him closer to me, deepening the kiss and our connection.

He pulls away, breaking the contact between us much sooner than I would have liked, but considering we're in a bar; it's probably for the best. He starts to lean forward and I think he's going to kiss me again. He leans in farther, his warm breath ghosting over my ear, my body buzzing from the brief contact. "Thanks for the beer," he whispers before placing a gentle kiss on that sweet spot just below my earlobe, my skin tingling where his lips caressed my heated skin. He pulls back, winks at me, picks up the pint glass, turns around, and walks away. Leaving me a panting, breathless, wet, turned on mess.

"Holy fucking hotness, Batman," Cress says from beside to me, I totally forgot she was here. "I think I need a cold shower after that."

"You and me both," I stammer, as I watch him walk away. And I can say, his ass is just as fine as the rest of him.

"You going to go after that hot piece of ass?"

I shake my head. "Nope, if he wants me, he can chase me."

"That's my girl!" Cress shouts. "Dude, two shots of whiskey…please," she hollers to the bartender. Throwing her arm around my shoulder, she leans in and whispers, "Let's loosen you up for Mr. Outlander over there."

Shaking my head, I laugh. "Jamie is Scottish. Flynn is Irish."

"Whatever!" she says in a Cher from *Clueless* tone. "They both end in 'ish, now let's liquor you up so you grow a pair of lady balls and go home with that Hottie McHotterson, and get you past third base AAAND maybe I can go home with his Channing Tatum look-alike friend?" She raises her eyebrows suggestively at me as she nods toward the pair. Turning around, I see they are both extraordinarily hot and both of them are looking our way.

Shaking my head, a laugh escapes me. I can't believe: A. That just kiss just happened and B. That Cress just said that to me, but at the same time I can because, well, it's Cress. Crass Cress was her nickname at school, and it's stuck ever since. All these years later, she still lives up to the nickname. While she orders another round of beers and shots for us, my mind drifts to a dirty place with Dr. Flynn Kelly. Pressing my thighs together to ease the throb, I take a sip of my drink. Glancing over my shoulder, I find he's still staring at me. My heart rate increases when I see him grin at me.

Turning back to face the bar, I purse my lips and wonder if I can do it.

Can I go home with a complete stranger?

Can I have a one-night stand?

This is new territory for me, but if I'm being honest with myself, I think I want to.

Looking back over my shoulder, Flynn winks at me. With that one action, it cements my decision; I'm going home with a hot Irishman tonight.

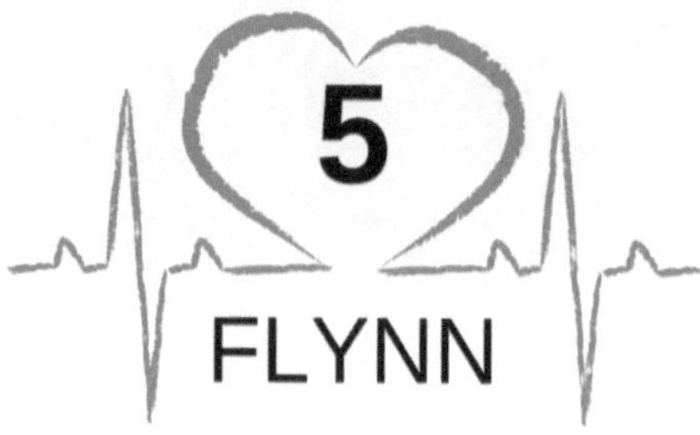

My eyes have been locked on Avery since we walked in. Even when she smacked me in the nuts, it didn't deter my want, my need, my hunger for this woman. From my seat, I watch as she sashays across the bar, her hips seductively swaying from side to side with each step she takes. My eyes rake over her body, and fuck me; this woman is stunning. What adds to her allure is she doesn't realize how goddamn sexy she is. She turns down the corridor toward the restrooms and out of sight. Waiting a few moments so I don't look like a creeper, I retrace her steps, but rather than heading down the corridor to the restrooms, I hide in an alcove off to the side, waiting for her to return. Ready to pounce and take what's mine.

Leaning against the wall, I feel her presence before I

see her. Looking up, I smile as I watch her walk toward me. Before she steps out into the main bar, I grab her wrist and pull her toward me. Spinning her around, she gasps in shock as I cocoon her between the brick wall and my body. Caging her in, I place my hands either side of her head and we stare at one another. The light is dim but as I gaze into her hazel eyes, I see them fill with desire when she realizes it's me. She opens her mouth to speak but I cover her lips with mine, devouring her mouth in a searing X-rated kiss. She slides her hands over my shoulders and runs her fingers up into the hair at the nape of my neck, just like she did earlier. The sensation causes my cock to twitch and harden between us, poking her in the belly. My heart is rapidly racing within my chest, it feels like it's going to break through my body. I've never had a reaction like this before from a kiss, I can only imagine what it will be like when I fuck her.

Her kisses become hurried, she wraps her leg around my thigh, shamelessly rubbing herself on me as we continue to devour each other's mouth. Our hands roam and explore each other's bodies over our clothes. The temperature in the alcove rising by the second, she moans into our kiss when I slide my hand down her arm and across her chest. Cupping her breast with my palm, I gently squeeze her soft plump mound. Sliding my hand inside the V of her dress and under the material of her bra, I massage and knead her breast. Her body heats under my touch with the skin on skin contact. With my other hand, I graze it ever so slowly down her body, her sexy as fucking sin body; a body I cannot wait to see sprawled naked in my bed. Gripping the hem of her dress, I slide my hand up her leg that's not wrapped around me. Skimming my finger over the top of her barely-there panties, I slide my fingers between her thighs and cup her mound.

"Please," she murmurs into my mouth, as she opens she legs wider for me. "Finger fuck me," she breathlessly growls, circling her hips onto my thigh and hand. This is an unexpected turn of events, but I'm more than happy to oblige. If I'm honest, I thought she would be quiet and meek, I like this sexy vixen side of her.

Teasing her, I run my finger in circles over her soaked panties. "Please," she cries again. The pleading in her voice does all kinds of things to me. With a forceful tug, I tear her panties off of her, the material disintegrating under the force. I thrust two fingers inside of her. They enter with ease due to her wetness. She gasps at the sudden intrusion and when I slide a third digit in with the others, she begins to ride my hand. Grinding herself against my digits. Moaning at the friction, I continue to slide my fingers in and out of her hot wet channel. My tongue mimics the motion of my hand within her mouth.

"Fuck my fingers, lass," I whisper against her lips, resting my forehead against hers, as I continue to thrust my fingers in and out of her. Her hips circling and thrusting in sync with my movements.

"Yes," she mewls.

Pulling back, I watch her face as euphoria radiates through her body. Her eyes are closed, she's lost in her pleasure. Her body tenses and she begins to scream. Slamming my lip against hers, I kiss her deeply and swallow her orgasmic cries. Her body violently shuddering as she rides out her orgasm.

She lowers her leg and stares up at me. Her cheeks are a sexy shade of 'I just came' pink. She's breathing heavily. Her chest heaving as she catches her breath.

With my eyes locked on hers, I lift my fingers to my mouth and slide them in. Licking and sucking them clean. A moan breaks free when the taste of her sweet sweet nectar hits my tongue. Her eyes widen at my motion. "You have the sweetest tasting pussy, Avery. A man could become addicted, and after just one taste, I'm addicted. I want and need more." Her cheeks darken at my words. With my eyes locked on hers, I slip my fingers back into my mouth and suck up the last remnants of her orgasm.

Leaning into her, I whisper, "Avery, I'm going to take you home now and I'm going to eat you, suck you, and fuck you repeatedly. All.Night.Long." Emphasizing the last three words.

Nibbling on her earlobe, I pull my head back and stare at her. "Nod if you agree." She blinks rapidly before slightly nodding her head.

Without saying a word, I grab her hand and pull her out into the main bar area. Walking over to her friend, I tell her Avery is coming with me. I don't give either of them a chance to speak. Picking up her purse, I drag her out of the bar after stopping to tell Preston to make sure her friend gets home safely. He nods his head with a sly grin, and I leave the Tavern with Avery for a night I'm not going to forget anytime soon.

6

AVERY

Holy shit, I'm leaving the Tavern with a sexy as sin doctor.

A doctor who I just let finger fuck me in said tavern.

A doctor who I *asked* to finger fuck me said tavern.

What is this man doing to me? And why do I like it so much?

This isn't me. I'm shy, reserved, and quiet. I don't leave bars with men I just met, or let them do things like *that* to me in public. From the limited conversation I've had with him, I can tell we are polar opposites but I'm drawn to him like a moth to a flame, and for once in my life, I don't care if I get burned. In fact, bring it on.

As I slip into his car, I lean back into the soft leather seat and a laugh escapes me.

"What's so funny?" he asks, as he hungrily stares down at me.

Gazing up at him, I shake my head. "It's nothing." If he knew what I was thinking, he'd pull me out of his car so fast my head would spin. He'd leave me standing in the parking lot alone and screech out of here as if he was driving in the Indianapolis 500. I keep my mouth shut because I don't want that. I want him to do exactly as he said. I want Flynn Kelly to fuck me, suck me and devour me all night long.

My mind drifts to all the sexy and dirty things I want him to do me. My body trembles at what I hope is ahead for me tonight. While I am lost in thought, he closes my door and climbs into the driver's seat. He starts the car and turns to look at me. His gaze is hungry and the desire I have for him skyrockets. I've never felt like this before. Brushing my hair behind my ear, I give him a shy smile. In return, he gives me a panty-melting grin and then I remember I'm no longer wearing any, he ripped mine off me back at the bar. Leaning across the center console, he threads his fingers into my hair, pulls me toward him, and presses his lips against mine. The kiss starts out gentle but quickly becomes heated, and he's now tongue fucking my mouth; I think this is my new favorite pastime.

Breaking the kiss, he huskily says, "I can't wait to have your sexy ass lips wrapped around my cock."

Between my thighs throbs at the thought and a slight moan slips free. He grins, and turns his attention back to job at hand, getting us back to his place as quickly as possible. He puts the car into reverse and we leave The Fat Fox for his place...and a night I'm sure to remember for the rest of my life.

Ten minutes later, he pulls into the underground

parking garage for his building. Coming to a stop in his parking spot, he puts the car in park and turns off the ignition. Nerves start to kick in but the desire and need coursing through my body pushes them away. Turning to look over at him, I notice him swallow deeply. He must sense me staring at him because he turns to face me and from the look on his face, any thoughts and all fears dissipate.

Our eyes lock.

The air around us thickens..

My heart races, faster than ever before.

A force beyond my control over takes my body and I climb across the console and into his lap. Gripping his cheeks in my palms, I press my lips to his. I gyrate my hips on his hardening cock and I kiss the life out of him.

Just like he did to me, I fuck his mouth with my tongue and rub myself on his growing cock.

I've never been this brazen before, but this man brings out a side of me I never knew existed. A side I kind of like. Sexy vixen Avery is fun. He slides his hands up the back of my thighs and grips my ass, squeezing tightly as we continue to devour each other. A sound from nearby pulls us apart. Both of us breathing heavily. Panting.

"Let's take this upstairs," he growls.

Words elude me in this moment, so I nod my head in agreement when fear begins to creep in. *What in the hell am I doing?* Climbing out of the driver's side door, since I was in his lap, I wait for him to step out. He hands me my purse and after closing the car door, he links his fingers with mine and a calmness washes over me. That one simple touch instantly put me at ease. Silently we walk toward the elevators. My eyes keep sneaking peeks at him. I cannot believe this is happening. As we wait for the elevator to arrive, I dig my nails into my palm to see if this is real. To see if I'm dreaming. I feel the pressure of my nail against my skin so I know this is real. I'm not dreaming. I really did leave a bar with someone I just met and I'm about to have my first one-night stand.

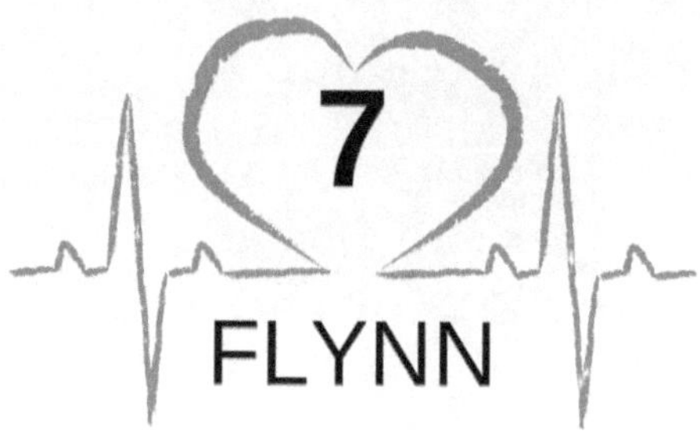

What is this woman doing to me?

I nearly fucked her in the underground parking garage, thank God that noise spooked us. I don't want anyone seeing her naked. I know that's rich, considering not thirty minutes ago I was finger fucking her at the bar, but it was dark and we were in a secluded alcove. Here? Anyone could have walked past and seen. I'm not an exhibitionist per se but I'm one hundred and ten percent sure Avery isn't. Sure, I've fucked in the on-call room and in my car up at the bluff when I was in med school, but never so brazenly out in public like this.

We exit my car and as I step toward Avery, I take a deep calming breath. Lacing my fingers with hers, a euphoric feeling washes over me and I pull her toward the elevator, eager to get her upstairs and naked beneath me. Pressing the call button, I stare at her out of the corner of my eye and as we wait, I notice her fidgeting. She's nervous and by the tinge of pink in her cheeks, aroused. Her nerves add to her sexiness, and I cannot wait for what's about to happen when we get upstairs. The doors open, I drop my hand to her lower back and usher her into the waiting elevator. Reaching over, I push the button for the penthouse and look back at her. Her mouth drops and her eyes pop wide open at this revelation. Placing my finger under her chin, I lift her gaze up to meet mine. We stare intently at one another as the elevator begins its journey to the top floor.

Our eyes are locked on one another and just like each time I look at her, something passes between us, it's an unspoken word of desire. The air in the car around us thickens and once again, my heart is racing profusely. At the same time, we step toward one another and our lips meet in a searing hot kiss. Our hands roam and caress. Our hearts beat erratically against each other. Blood and lust race through our veins. We both moan as our wanton sexual tension envelops us.

Sliding my hands down and around to her backside, I squeeze her ass and tap. She jumps up and wraps her legs around my waist. The feeling of her wrapped around me is far better than how I imagined it. She unabashedly grinds herself on me. My cock presses painfully against my zipper at the friction. Wrapping her arms around my neck, her breasts press into my chest, her taut pointy nipples poking me through our clothes. *I can't wait to suckle them,* I think to myself as the elevator doors open. Stepping out into the penthouse foyer, I walk us toward my front door. Pressing her into the mahogany, I dig in my pocket for my keys. If I was thinking clearly, I would have already had them out, but with her sexy body pressing against me, my thoughts were preoccupied.

With the keys finally in my hand, I take a step back, slip the metal into the lock, and unlock the door. Our lips remain sealed and my grip on her tightens as I maneuver the door open without dropping her. Multitasking with a goddess like Avery in my arms is harder than you'd think. My brain is fried, all the blood in my body is currently throbbing between my thighs, my cock harder than it's ever been before.

Stepping over the threshold, I stride into my living room and lower her to the sofa. She lies back on the chocolate brown leather and her glossy brown locks fan out behind her, creating a chocolate halo beneath her. She's fucking gorgeous. My eyes rake over her body from head to toe as I memorize each and every inch of her. "Avery, you are so fucking stunning."

Resting my knee on the sofa between her spread thighs, I slide up between her legs, gently pressing into her sex. At the same time, I skim my fingertip up her leg, her skin prickling with goose pimples under my touch. My hand keeps going and I trace the silky material up her side, across her stomach, before circling my finger around her breast. Her nipple hardens under my touch, pressing against the material of her dress.

Leaning down, I cocoon her beneath me and nuzzle into the side of her neck and massage her breast, pulling the taut peak of her nipple between my thumb and forefinger. Wishing there was no material between us. She moans as I nibble along her jaw. Throwing her head back into the cushion, she gives me full access to her neck. She threads her fingers in my hair, gently scraping her nails along my scalp. My cock twitches with each scratch.

Gazing down at her, I smirk before I lower my head and cover her mouth with mine. We kiss and lose ourselves in each other. Without warning, she flips us over —wow, she's a lot stronger than I thought—and straddles me. She grins down at me and winks. Gripping the hem of her dress, she lifts it over her head and drops it to the rug below. Leaving her in only her sexy as fuck, lace strapless bra that is doing nothing to hide her nipples. She's bare, as her panties are shredded and on the floor in the alcove back at the Tavern.

Lifting my hands, I gently caress her breasts as she rotates her hips on my cock. Pulling the lace cup down, I pinch her nipple between my thumb and forefinger, finally skin on skin contact. Her skin is silky soft, I cannot wait to burrow my face between her tits, licking, sucking, and marking her delicate skin. Her head drops back as I continue to fondle her breasts. They felt great in my hands through her dress but with nothing between us now, they are even better. Lifting myself up into a sitting position, I press my face into the valley of her breasts. Breathing her in, I groan, she even smells amazing. Licking up the side of her breast, I take one of her stiff pink peaks into my mouth. Sucking deeply, my tongue swirls around the tip before I suck again, gently biting down.

"Flynn," she huskily moans, as she presses my head farther into her bosom. Scrapping her nails across the back of my scalp, I moan against her flesh. Pulling my head from her breast, she grips my cheeks in her palms. Lifting my gaze from her breasts, I stare into her eyes. "Fuck me, Flynn," she pants as she tears at my shirt, buttons fly everywhere as she tugs the material down my arms. Throwing it to the floor, she shuffles back and begins to work on my pants. Without knocking her off me, I manage to free my cock and slip on a condom. She discards her bra and hungrily stares down at me. She bites and licks her bottom lip, and it's the sexiest thing I've ever seen. The only barrier between us now, nothing. She's gloriously naked on my lap and I cannot wait to slide my dick inside of her.

Gripping her sides, I lift her up and shuffle back onto the couch. She's kneeling across my lap. I can smell her pussy, I lick my lips. Her mouth drops open in shock as I slide my finger down her slit. She's soaked, spreading her wetness around, she lifts up on her knees and slowly shimmies forward and lowers herself onto me. We both moan as my cock slides into her wet folds. Her pussy hugs my cock tightly as she seats herself fully on me. With her eyes locked on mine, she slides herself up and down my rigid shaft. Gripping my shoulders tightly, her nails dig into my skin as she rides me like a stallion.

My left hand kneads her ass; squeezing and massaging her cheek. My other hand slides around her tiny waist and up to her breasts. Massaging gently, I tug on her nipple and pinch. Alternating back and forth between the two. "Flynnnnnnn," she moans, as I continue to fondle her breasts; they fit my hands perfectly. I can't wait to press my face into them again and that's exactly what I do. Leaning forward, I press her gorgeous tits together and lower my face between her plump mounds. I lick and suck her breasts. Gently biting her nipple, she moans and throws her head back. She runs her hands up into her hair, turning her head into her arms as she slides up and down my dick. We thrust our hips back and forth and I continue to devour her breasts. While I suck one nipple, I massage and squeeze the other. Repeating the motion over and over. She moans and groans as pleasure envelops us both. She makes the most amazing sound as her climax builds, a mixture between a wail and scream. The sound reverberates deep within me, pushing me to the edge.

"Avery, fuck," I groan, I'm teetering on the edge but I can't come. Not until she does. *She has to come before me*, I chant to myself over and over. She clenches me tighter and tighter with each thrust.

"I'm close," she cries.

Our eyes find one another and we stare deep into each other's souls as we thrust back and forth.

In and out.

Up and down.

Our bodies moving in sync. My balls tighten and I will myself not to come. *Not yet. Not yet*, I continue to chant. She slides her hand between us and flicks her clit, this sensation causes her to tense and shudder around me. Her body violently shakes and she screams, "Yes! Yes! Yes!" as her climax detonates. This sets me off and together we explode, screaming in ecstasy as we ride out our orgasm.

Our bodies quivering as the pleasure endorphins sore throughout us, she collapses forward, pressing her tits into my chest. Her hair shrouding me as we both breathe heavily and come down from our orgasmic high. She lifts her head and stares at me, her lips lift in a shy smile. "That was…"

"Yep," I say, as I tuck her hair behind her ear, cupping

her face in my palm. Something passes between us, she leans forward and kisses me. This kiss is different, it's not as frenzied as our earlier ones but it's just as poignant. With her still straddling me, I remove the condom, tie it off and drop it to the carpet. Gripping her hips, I flip her on to her back. I settle between her legs and we make out like horny teenagers on a Saturday night.

She reaches around and grabs one of the condoms I dropped earlier. "Please," she murmurs into the kiss. Breaking the connection, I see what's in her fingers. Taking the rubber from her, I sheath my cock and stare down at her. She spreads her legs wide and that's all the invitation I need. With a flick of my hips, I slide inside her again. Even though I just came harder than ever before, I'm ready and raring to go once again. We fall into a rhythm, thrusting our hips back and forth. Our bodies and lips moving in sync. Our tongues caress one another and quicker than I would have liked, we both tumble over the orgasmic cliff once again.

Wrapping my arms under her, I lift her up and she wraps her limbs tightly around me. Walking us into my bedroom, I pull back the duvet and place her down on the bed. Sliding in next to her, we face one another and chat. I tell her about growing up in Ireland. She tells me about, Baylor, her twin sister. I get the feeling something is up there but I don't push it. I want to keep tonight light and fun. We continue to swap stories into the wee hours of the morning. She makes me laugh, and boy do we laugh. We share information with one another like I do with Preston; never have I done that before after a hookup, but Avery Evans is more than just a hookup. I want more with this woman. Tomorrow morning over breakfast, I'll broach that subject, because right now, her eyes are drooping and she's ready for sleep.

Pulling her into my side, she rests her head on my chest and throws her leg over mine. We blissfully drift off to sleep, wrapped in each other's arms. This is an amazing end to what was a horrendous day and I cannot wait for tomorrow.

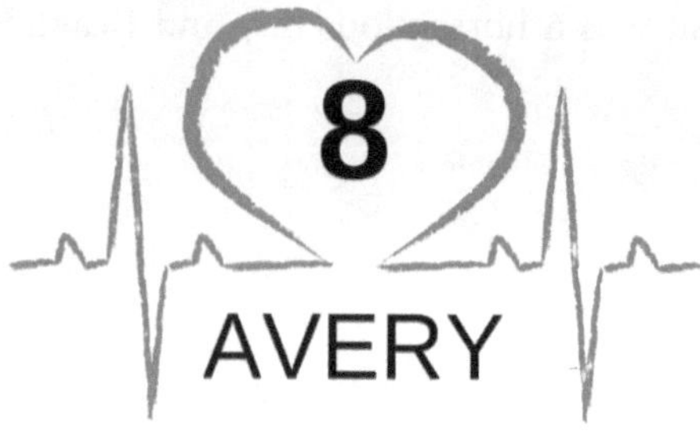

OPENING MY EYES, I'M DISORIENTATED FOR A MOMENT. Blinking a few times, the room comes into view, but when I glance around I don't recognize anything. The walls are a dark gray, the furniture is dark, and the ever so soft bed is huge and isn't mine.

Then I remember.

Memories of last night come rushing back to me. My clit throbs as they play back in slow motion through my mind, my body tingling as I recall each and every deliciously sexy moment from last night.

A noise from beside me snaps me back to the present, and my gaze drifts to the side. I'm met with a muscular back and the hint of a butt cheek—a gorgeously firm butt cheek, if my recollections from when said cheeks were firmly pressed in my palms is correct. My eyes move north and I get a sudden urge to lean over and lick down his spine and bite his butt cheek.

What the hell? That's not me. I don't think dirty thoughts like this. Hell, I don't usually do ANY of the things I have done with this man. This man makes me do things I never in a million years would ever consider doing, but with how my body feels right now, I'm so glad he pulled me out of my comfort zone.

Rolling to my back, I stare up at the ceiling and then it happens. Panic starts to build within and a sudden urge to flee overtakes me—there's the shy, conservative, rule abiding Avery that I know. Like seriously, I'm an elementary school teacher, I don't pick up sexy as sin doctors in a bar...or go home with them. Nor do I let sexy as sin demigod's finger fuck me in public or make out and dry hump them in their car. Or have hours and hours of mind-blowing, out of the world, amazing sex. Or have naked deep and meaningful conversations at stupid a.m. with a complete stranger.

Fuck, fuck, fuck, I have to get out of here.

Movement from next to me pauses my racing thoughts. It seems during my mini mental breakdown freak-out, Flynn woke up and rolled over to face me. He's staring at me and even with a sleepy look on his face, he is the most gorgeous man I have ever laid my eyes upon. His gaze bores into me, my skin heating from the intense desire in his eyes. His gaze calms me and pushes my freak-out to the side, especially when his hand slips below the sheet and slides between my thighs. Like the whore I've turned into, I spread my legs for him, inviting him to do anything he wants to me. He rubs up and down my lips. Instantly I'm wet—whore—and his finger slides with ease into my sex. I moan at the friction and press myself into his hand. My eyes droop closed and my head rolls back on the pillow. I need more. I want more. I want Flynn like I need my next breath. *What is with this man and his magical fingers?*

My legs spread wider and I turn my head to face him, we stare one another as he continues to finger me. Pleasure builds deep in my belly. He thrusts two fingers inside, I moan in delight and close my eyes. My back arches and I whimper in ecstasy. He leans over and presses his lips to mine. His tongue licks along my lips, before sliding in and out of my mouth, in sync with his fingers between my legs. Before long, I explode around his fingers. Screaming as pleasure rumbles throughout my body.

Flynn removes his fingers, and he traces his fingertip along my bottom lip before bringing them to his lips. He slips them into his mouth and sucks. My mouth waters at seeing this. Licking my bottom lip, I taste myself for the first time. It's tart and tangy, not what I expected. He grins at me as he tugs the sheet off my body. He grabs my hand and places it on his cock, his rock-hard cock. Gripping his dick in my palm, I squeeze and flick my wrist up and down. The pad of my finger slides over the tip, spreading the leaking precum around. Our eyes are locked on one another as I jerk him off. He grips my hand and halts my movements. "I'm going to come if you keep that up."

Lifting to my knees, I shimmy down the bed, and with my eyes on him, I take him into my mouth, the tip hitting the back of my throat. Hollowing my cheeks, I suck and pump his cock. Repeating the motion over and over. His breathing becomes labored. His body stiffens and then I feel the first burst of hot salty cum hit the back of my throat. I suck and lick every last drop. I've never been into head before, but this man seems to bring me out of my comfort zone in many different sexual ways.

Pulling back, his cock pops out of my mouth. He beckons me forward with his finger in a come-hither motion. Straddling his legs, ever so slowly I crawl up his body. Kissing, licking, and nipping every ripple along his perfect body as I go. Licking up his neck, I straddle his waist and sit up. I stare down at him and smile. "You beckoned me?" I huskily say, not recognizing my sexed-up voice or this sex vixen version of me.

Flynn sits up, wraps his arms around my lower back and presses his face into my breasts. He attacks them with vigor. Each nip and suck sending shock waves straight between my thighs. My head drops back and I lose myself to the pleasure ricocheting throughout my body. My hips begin rocking back and forth; his cock hardens between us. Sliding my hand down, I grip his dick and begin to stroke. When he's hard as steel, I lift myself onto my knees and I slam myself down on him. "Fuuuuck!" I shout, as I impale myself fully on him, he's deeper than any cock has been before. He lifts his head from between my breasts. "Condom," he growls.

"I'm on the pill," I say, my eyes locked on his. There's a hint of indecision in his eyes. "I'm clean. I promise."

"I'm clean too." He smiles at me and nods his head.

Nodding in return, I begin to ride him. I've never not used protection before, I can feel every ridge on his cock, without the latex barrier it's much more intense. I grunt and groan as pressure builds within. My hips piston back and forth. Flynn thrusts up from below. He's so deep it hurts but at the same time, it's the most exquisite feeling ever. His cock is deep inside, it feels like he hits my cervix each time; it's ohh so delicious.

"Flynn," I croon, as I grip his shoulders for leverage and increase my thrusts. We thrash back and forth. The only sounds in the room are our heavy breathing and skin slapping on skin. Out of nowhere my orgasm detonates. I scream as my climax peaks, euphoria pulsates through my muscles from head to toe. My body tingling, never have I had such an intense orgasm like this before.

Flynn's body tenses against mine. His arms tighten around me and I feel him release inside me. He grunts and squeezes me as he climaxes. Collapsing back onto the bed, I fall with him. He gingerly traces his fingertip along my spine. I'm completely sated and well fucked, I drift off to sleep lying across his chest.

My full bladder wakes me, I don't want to move but if I don't it won't be pretty. Slipping slip out of bed, I walk into his en suite bathroom. It's clean and masculine, like the rest of his place. Gray tiles, white vanity. Even his towels are a charcoal gray. After using the toilet, I step to the sink and wash my hands. Glancing in the mirror, I don't recognize the person staring back at me. My cheeks are flushed, I feel relaxed and invigorated. Then I think about last night, and this morning, and with those thoughts in the forefront of my mind, I begin to freak out, again. *Shit, shit, shit. What have I done?* Conservative Avery is here, this is the Avery I'm used to and the one I know. No longer is the sexy confident vixen from last night present. Shy awkward me has returned, and she needs to get out of here and she needs to leave now.

Poking my head into the bedroom, I thank the heavens when I see Flynn is still sleeping soundly. Quietly tiptoeing out, I quickly exit his room. My heart is racing and it feels loud, like a herd of elephants trampling through the safari park. Stepping into the living room, I find my dress by the sofa. Picking it up, I slip it over my head. Then the clean freak in me appears. Picking up his discarded clothes, I fold them neatly in a pile and place them on the coffee table. Bending down, I pick up my bra, grab my shoes and clutch, and exit his place.

As I wait for the elevator, I sigh in relief that I escaped without being caught. My mind is a jumbled mess right now, and I'm ever so thankful I don't need to do the awkward morning/afternoon-after chitchat I've heard about. *How do people do this all the time?*

The elevator doors open and I press the button for the lobby. Shoving my bra into my bag, I slip on my shoes, and cringe when I realize I have no panties. I've just slipped my shoes on when the doors open to the lobby. Exiting, I race across marble floor, my heels clicking on the tiles loudly, basically announcing my walk of shame to the empty lobby, except for the concierge and doorman. Lowering my head down in mortification, I quickly race through the lobby and push the door open before the doorman can do it. Stepping out to the street, my heart is racing in my chest. I've never done the walk of shame before, and I don't ever wish to feel like this again. Looking to the street, I smile when I see someone getting out of a taxi.

Smiling at them, I carefully climb in—don't want a Britany vag flash—and give the driver my address. Sitting back in my seat, I rest my head against the headrest and let out the breath I hadn't realized I was holding. Grabbing my phone, I call Cress. She picks up on the second ring. "Afternoon, hussy."

"Morning," I reply, as I glance at my watch and realize it's almost one in the afternoon.

"Sooo…" she prompts, "how was your night?"

"Good," I say, as memories of last night play in vivid sexy high definition color in my mind, and my traitorous body zings with delight.

"Good, that's all I get good?"

"Yep. I'm in a taxi on my way home right now." Pausing, I purse my lips. I sigh and whine, "Cress—"

"I'll be there when you get home." I love that she knows what I need right now.

"Thank you," I whisper, but she's already hung up. I'm ever so grateful to have a friend like her because I really, really need her right now. I need her to help me compartmentalize everything that has eventuated in the last twelve hours.

Leaning back in the taxi, I close my eyes and then I lift my head and shoot upright. *Holy shit, I had an out of this world one-night stand and then I snuck out. I'm such a whore.* "Fucking hell," I mumble, as I lean my head against the side window and close my eyes. I feel so dirty, so skanky right now, but at the same time so alive and liberated.

Doubt starts to creep in, maybe I shouldn't have snuck out like I did but really, what other choice did I have? It's not like I'll ever see the sexy as sin doctor again.

With a smile on my face, I open my eyes and reach out to the side. I need to hold her against me as I wake up, but I'm met with nothing. My hand feels a cold sheet beneath it, turning my head to the side, I frown when I see the bed empty. *She must be in the bathroom,* I think to myself when I see the door closed. Lying back down, I stare at the ceiling and find myself grinning from ear to ear. Last night was beyond my wildest dreams amazing. I've slept with a lot of women but Avery Evans, fuck me, she strides to the top of the list.

It's been a while now, and she hasn't returned. "Avery?" I call out as I sit up in bed. Walking naked to the bathroom door, I knock. "Ave lass, are you okay?" Again I'm met with silence, pushing the door open I find it empty. Turning around, I walk into the living room and find it empty. Stepping around the sofa, I see her dress is gone, and my clothes are folded neatly on the coffee table. And then it hits me, she snuck out. "Motherfucker," I groan, running my hands through my hair. Dropping down to the sofa, I rest my elbows on my knees and dejectedly sigh. She didn't seem like the person who would fuck and chuck, then again, I know dick all about her. Sure we chatted before falling asleep in the wee hours of the morning, but the topics we discussed were nothing serious.

Leaning back into the sofa, I smile as a vision of Avery riding me in this exact spot last night flashes before me. I can still smell her pussy, her sweet sweet pussy. My cock hardens thinking about her taste. My mouth waters and I imagine the sounds she made when she came. "Fuuuuck!" I growl as I grip my cock and begin to stroke. The sound of her purring like the sex kitten she is plays over and over on a loop in my mind. My grip on my cock tightens, my tugs hurried, and soon I'm spraying cum all over my stomach.

Collapsing back onto the couch, I lie here breathing heavily and think about the dark-haired angel who got away. Heading back into my bedroom, I climb into the shower and wash the remnants of my self-love away. Climbing out, I dry off and decide to head back to the Tavern, maybe she'll be back there for a quiet beverage to end the weekend.

Calling Preston, he agrees to meet me there in an hour.

An hour later, I walk in and my eyes dart around the bar, but my raven-haired beauty isn't here. Preston is and he's got a grin on his face. "Hey," he says, as I sit across from him. Picking up his drink, I slam it back. "Rough night?" he cheekily questions.

"Amazing night. Rough afternoon." I reply, flagging down the waitress, I order myself a beer and another scotch for Preston.

"That's two extremes."

"That's how the last eighteen hours have gone."

"Huh?"

"Last night and this morning were amazing with Avery. We clicked, and not just between the sheets." I take sip of beer the waitress just delivered. "Well, I thought we clicked. When I woke up just after lunch, she was gone. No note. Nothing. The only reason I knew she was there was because she folded my clothes and left them on the coffee table."

"Huh?"

"Before she left, she folded my clothes that were left in the living room last night."

"At least she's neat," he teases, as he takes a sip of his drink.

"Not what I'm focusing on at the moment." Then it hits me, he was with her friend last night, "How did you go last night?" He shrugs his shoulders. "What does that mean?"

"It means I looked after the friend like you requested."

"Aaaaand?" I probe.

"And nothing. We had a drink after you guys left and then I dropped her home."

"Really? You didn't fuck her?"

"Nope, my dick stayed in my pants. By the sound of things, you had enough sex for the both of us last night and this morning."

Shrugging, my mind once again drifts to last night, especially when my eyes gravitate toward the hallway to the restrooms. Vividly, what went down between us in the alcove flashes before my eyes.

"So what are you going to do?" His question stumps me.

"No clue. Did you get the friends details at all?"

He shakes his head but from the look on his face, he's full of shit. Something happened last night, I'd bet my left nut on it. But I know Preston Knight; he will keep this secret to himself until he's ready to share. That's one of the things I love most about the guy, he is loyal to a T.

Not wanting to bring him down with my foul mood, I say goodbye and head home to bed. Lying in my bed, I think about Avery, the one who got away. She helped me get over my blue balls, but now, it's my mind that's all messed up.

10

AVERY

CRESS IS THE BESTEST FRIEND EVER. TWENTY MINUTES AFTER I arrive home, she turns up with wine, ice cream, and a gorgeous little girl. "Lexi, how you doing?"

"I'm good, Aunty A. I got to sleep at Nana's last night and then this morning, Mommy took me to the park and I got an ice cream."

"So I can see. What flavor did you get?"

"Mint chocolate chip."

"Yummo, my fav." Her face is all sticky and there's a chocolate splotch down the front of her *My Little Pony* shirt. At the moment, Lexi is obsessed with everything associated with that show. "You wanna watch some Pony while Mom and I chat in the kitchen?"

"Yessssss," she squeals in delight. She races into the

living room and pulls out her beanbag and settles in while I switch it on. The theme song starts and I walk into the kitchen to find that my uber awesome best friend has a glass of wine waiting for me.

"Okay, spill," she says, as she hands me a glass of wine.

Taking the wine from her, I take a huge gulp, followed by another. "Okay, Chuggy McChuggerson, slow down there," she teases, as she takes the glass from me and tops it up—see, bestest friend ever.

Looking to her, my freak-out erupts with vigor. Tears well in my eyes. My chest becomes tight. Breathing is difficult. "Cress, I'm a big fat whore," I cry as Cress envelops me in a hug and lets me cry into her shoulder. "I slept with him so many times and it was ducking amazing." We don't swear when Lex is around. "It was the best ducking sex of my life. I'm surprised I'm not waddling today. When he was asleep, I snuck out, and now I feel guilty for leaving him like that. I can't even apologize for being such a ducking whore. At least I folded his clothes before I left."

She pulls away, holding me at arm's length and pulls a confused face. "You folded his clothes?"

Nodding my head up and down, I confirm, "Yeah, when I slipped my dress back on, I picked his clothes up, folded them, and placed them neatly on the coffee table."

Cress laughs at me. "Only you would have a one-night stand and then clean before leaving."

"Cress," I whine, "I'm a big fat whore."

"NO!," she shouts, wiping under my eyes with her thumb. "You are a sexy single gal, who had a fantabulous night ducking a hot guy."

"But—"

"NO! NO! NO! NO! NO!" she scolds. "Avery Evans,

look at me." I lift my gaze to hers. "One night of amazing sex does not make you a whore. Did he pay you?"

"No."

"Then by definition you are not a whore, maybe a skank but definitely not a whore."

"Takes a skank to know a skank."

And just like that, all my whore fears are erased, but now I feel guilty for leaving. "Stop with the guilts for sneaking out," Cress says, giving me the mom eye she has down pat.

"How did you know?"

"I know all your tics," she nonchalantly says, she hands me my wine and this time, I take a small sip and savor the crispness of the white. "Now, listen to me, I will only say this once. You will not call yourself a whore for having fantabulous sex. You will not feel guilty for sneaking out like the harlot who I'm finally able to call my best friend. I'm proud, wee skankhopper. We, well you, are going to put last night with the sexy Scottish—"

"Irish."

"You are going to put last night with that sexy Irish doctor into the flick bank and move on."

"I knew you were my best friend for a reason. In half—"

"Three quarters," she teases.

"Fine, in three-quarters of a glass of wine, you've eased my fears and I feel like me again."

"Happy to be of service. Now, I want all the sexy filthy details."

Shaking my head, I take a sip. "Nope, last night is firmly locked away in my, what did you call it?"

"Flick bank," she offers.

"Yes, flick bank. Last night is safely locked away there.

Now, I'm going to have a shower 'cause I smell like sex. You can order dinner and then we can watch *My Little Pony* with Lexi."

"Can't we watch something else?" she cries.

"Do you want to enrage your daughter?"

"Fair point."

With my wine glass in hand, I step out of the kitchen to go have a shower. Turning around, I pop my head back in, and say, "Cress, thanks for being you and calming me down."

"You are most welcome, babe. It's not often I get to rescue you, so it's nice to repay the favor for once…even if you won't spill the sexy schmexy details with your BFF."

"Love you," I call out, as I walk down the hallway to my room.

Cress really is the best friend I could ask for. Baylor used to share that spot with Cress, but in the last few weeks she's changed. I don't like the person she's turning into, not that I've really seen her. She's been MIA more times than not. I really hope she's okay, but my gut and twin instinct tell me she's spiraling out of control and she's about to crash and burn.

…three weeks later

I'VE TAKEN AN EXTRA SHIFT IN THE ER AND I'M SERIOUSLY regretting it. It's insanely busy today, and not just because we are short-staffed. It must be a full moon or something has been slipped into the water supply, because the cases today are batshit crazy and the patients all seem to be angry assholes with asshole family members or friends with them. With another chart in hand, I pull back the curtain, step in, look to the bed, and pause midstep. My eyes pop wide open when I see whom my next patient is… looks like picking up this extra shift wasn't such a bad idea after all. With a grin on my face, I casually say, "Hi." Stopping at the end of her bed. My eyes rake up and down her body. My eyes land on hers, but something is amiss.

"Well, hello there, handsome," she replies, her eyes lighting up but they aren't as vibrant as I remember and her hair seems lighter, but the lighting in here sucks and it has been three weeks since I last saw her. "Who knew hurting myself could be a good thing," she says, her voice deeper than I recall.

"How are you?" I ask, not the question I should be asking right now, but this woman has constantly been on my mind for the last three weeks, hell, I've even dreamed about her.

My eyes are locked on hers and my mind drifts to our night of unbridled passion together.

The moaning.

The groaning.

The thrusting.

The taste of her pussy.

The out of this world fucking.

The sound of our skin slapping together.

And then I remember she skipped out on me the next day.

Normally I don't care, but there's something about Avery that makes me want more. I felt a connection with her, and I know she did too. We meshed together in every way possible, and not just between the sheets. In amongst our marathon fuckfest, we had a deep and meaningful conversation that left me wanting more. I've never felt that before, and then she gave me my first taste of being fucked and chucked.

Shaking my head, I realize she's been talking but I have no clue about what she just said. Nodding my head, so I don't look like a complete idiot, I step to the side of the bed and place my hand on her calf, lifting up the ice pack. The spark that was there the other weekend when we touched is gone. I deflate a little on the inside, I really thought there was something between us, I guess there isn't anything there after all. Before I get a chance to ask a question, the curtain is pulled back. "Seriously, Bay, you are such a klutz at times."

That voice. My skins prickles at the sound of that melodic voice. My head snaps up and I spin around. For the second time in as many minutes, my mouth drops open in disbelief.

"Flynn."

"Avery."

We both say at the same time.

"Wwww…what are you doing here?" she stammers, her cheeks flushing as she stares at me.

"I work here." My eyes rake over her body. It seems my memory deceived me, Avery is more fucking gorgeous than I remember.

We continue to stare at one another. The intensity in her gaze causes my mind to flit back to our fucktastic night together.

Her head thrown back in ecstasy.

Her skin glistening with sweat.

Her gorgeous legs wrapped around my waist.

Her beautiful tits that fit perfectly in my hands.

The sexy sound she makes as she crashes over the orgasmic cliff.

My cock twitches at the memory.

The sound of her doppelgängers voice snaps me back to the present. "You two know each other?"

"No."

"Yes."

We each say.

We continue to stare at one another. I can't believe it's her. I'm being highly unprofessional right at this moment by ignoring my patient, but Avery is here. My Avery is standing in cubicle three. She's in front of me, in the flesh, but she's also lying on the bed beside me.

What the fuck?

My eyes dart back and forth between the two of them as I try and process this. A shrill voice breaks the silence, "Oh My God, you two totally fucked," comes from the Avery look-alike on the bed.

"Baylor, keep it down, we're in a hospital," Avery snarls. The girl in the bed sticks her tongue out at Avery. "Grow up, Sis, and have some class for God's sake. People don't need to hear you spouting this crap."

"Says the one who fucked Dr. Hottie McHotterson over here." She flicks her head in my direction. Her eyes wander over me and check me out from head to toe. It gives me the shivers and not in the good way. Her sister on the other hand, her sister causes my body to come alive just from her proximity. The woman in the bed, Baylor, her sister, licks her lips, but movement in my peripheral vision snaps my attention back over to Avery, beautiful shy Avery. She's my polar opposite in every way but I'm drawn to her like a magnet, by a force I cannot explain.

"Please ignore my sister," Avery says, as she steps closer to the end of the bed...and me. "She must have bumped her head as well as rolled her ankle." She lifts her hand and presses down on the ice pack covering her sister's ankle.

"Ouch, you bitch," Baylor whines, her face wincing in pain.

Glancing at the chart in my hands to calm myself, I look to my patient. "Baylor—"

"Bay," she interrupts and bats her eyelashes at me, clearly showing no respect for her sister. She totally knows something went on between us, yet she still flirts with me.

Ignoring her, I go on, "Baylor, I'm Dr. Kelly. Can you tell me what happened?"

She begins to speak but my eyes are locked on Avery. She's fucking gorgeous, I don't think I have ever met someone as stunning as her. Her shyness has returned and she's fidgeting by the end of the bed. Suddenly, I hear Baylor and I realize, once again, I didn't hear a word of what she just said. "Let's take a look," I interrupt her.

Placing the chart on the bed, I lift the ice pack and stare at her ankle. Her very swollen, bruised, and possibly broken ankle. Reaching out, I lightly touch her foot. She flinches and groans but the doctor in me knows she's exaggerating. "We'll get an X-ray and once we know what we're dealing with, we can go from there."

Exiting the cubicle, I walk over to the nurses' station and request an X-ray. I've just signed the X-ray request form when my skin prickles. I feel her approaching, turning around, I watch and stare as Avery hesitantly walks toward me. "Flynn, I'm—"

Shaking my head, I interrupt, "Not here and it's fine," I snap, harsher than I intended. She immediately shrinks into herself and I feel like a major dick. "Look, Avery. It's fine. If you'd prefer another doctor for your sister, I'm happy to do so. I don't want to make you uncomfortable." Where the fuck did that come from? I don't normally give a shit if someone is uncomfortable, but I really care about this woman and her feelings. She has me acting like a lovesick fool. Once again, I realize I tuned out and missed what she said. "Sorry, can you repeat that?"

She stares blankly at me. "There's no need to swap. It will just piss Bay off and a pissed-off Bay is never a good thing."

"Your sister, seems…nice," I say.

She knows I'm lying. "Mmmhmpf. That's not how I'd describe her but then again, I know my twin better than anyone." We continue to stare at one another. Everyone and everything around us fades into the background. My eyes are focused on the angel before me. The air around us zinging with electricity, just like it did three weeks ago. "Flynn, can we get a coffee sometime? It's the least I can do aft…"

"After you left me high and dry after our fucking amazing night together?" I say, arching my eyebrows.

She laughs, "Yeah, something like that." She steps toward me, rests her arm on my forearm, and lowers her voice. "I'm sorry I left how I did. I'm not normally that rude, but I've never done what we did before. In the reality of the daylight, I kinda freaked out."

"I was upset to find you gone when I woke up." Her face deflates. "Sorry, I didn't mean to upset you."

"How are you comforting me, when I'm the one…" She doesn't finish her sentence, she leaves it hanging. We stare at one another. All I see is Avery; shy gorgeous Avery. It's just the two of us, even though we are standing in the middle of the ER. That connection, that chemistry from the tavern and that night is still present. My eyes are locked on hers, my gaze bores deep into her soul. This woman who is the complete opposite to me has me wrapped around her finger. I'd do anything for more time with her. The saying opposites attract comes to mind and I'm one-hundred-percent attracted to her and definitely her opposite. I'm confident she's attracted to me too, but she's scared and I'm going to have to take control of the situation at hand.

Without thinking, I blurt, "Can I take you to dinner?"

AVERY

HOLY SHIT, HE WANTS TO TAKE ME TO DINNER.

What kind of guy does that? I sneak out like a thief in the night and he still wants to see me, is he crazy? I offered for us to get coffee, ease our way into something, and then he counters with dinner. *What the what?* Have I been sucked into an alternate universe? An alternate freaking universe where a sexy as hell Irish god, who also happens to be a doctor, wants me. Me? Avery Evans, plain-Jane teacher. He does remember that we had a one-night stand —a freaking amazing out of this world, porn worthy one-night stand—and then I snuck out. What are the freakin' odds that he turns out to be the doctor who treats my sister? And after ALL that, he still offers to take me out to dinner. *What the what? Is this guy nuts? Oh My God, don't think of his nuts 'cause that's near his thingy, his amazing thingy that gave me the most amazing pleasure E-V-E-R!*

I'm not sure what to do.

I've never been in this situation before.

What do I do?

What's the protocol when a one-night stand asks you out when you bump into one another?

Shy me wants to run and hide and forget I ever met Dr. Flynn Kelly.

Sex-bomb vixen me, who went home with him, really wants to go to dinner with him…and then have him for dessert. *Where the hell did that kinky thought come from? I don't think or say things like that.* Crap, what is this guy doing to me? Shit, he's staring at me, waiting for my reply.

Before I can stop myself I blurt out, "Sure, I'd love that." *What the hell, Evans?*

He smirks at me as he grabs a card off the counter and scribbles on the back of it. He hands it to me and just like before, when his fingers brush against mine, an electric current zaps between us. The air around us sizzles with desire and lust. He leans in and ever so softly kisses my cheek, my cheek tingles when his lips press against my skin.

"My cell's on the back. Call me to arrange dinner," he gruffly says, his voice sending shock waves through my body and igniting my soul. Before I can say anything, he steps away. Leaving me standing here like a lovesick fool with a grin on my face bigger than the Cheshire cat.

Grinning from ear to ear, I turn on my heel and walk back into the cubicle where Bay was, but it's empty. I'm guessing she's off for her X-ray so I take a seat and wait.

I'm thankful for the few moments of peace. My mind plays everything over and over.

Our night together.

The chats we had.

The morning together before I snuck out.

Our chat just now.

The peck on my cheek a moment ago.

Lifting my hand, I rest it where his lips were. A shudder runs though me. *I'm so scared when it comes to this man but at the same time, I'm intrigued and excited.* For the first time in my life, I want to be reckless and carefree. I'm going to go for it, what's the worst that could happen?

Sitting down on the chair on the corner, I wait for Bay to return. A short while later, the curtain pulls back and she returns. She plays the princess card and flirts excessively with the orderly. The fool goes out of his way to help her back onto the bed. Sitting in the corner, I shake my head and hold back a laugh.

Stretching my arms over my head, I stretch out my muscles and then lean back and continue watch the spectacle in front of me. How freakin' long does it take to get someone back into a bed? Finally, she's settled and the orderly leaves, pulling the curtain closed behind him. "You good?" I ask, when she looks over at me.

"What do you think?" she snaps at me, "My ankle is swollen. It looks like a melon is growing out the side of it, and I won't be able to head to Vegas with the girls this weekend. But at least there's a totally fuckable doctor on my case."

My blood boils when she says this. She knows something happened between Flynn and me, but in recent, typical Bay style, she's going to walk all over me. She's going to take what's mine; just like she did with my Princess Barbie when we were eight years old. Before I can tell her to back off, the curtain opens and Flynn steps in.

He looks to me and winks, my cheeks darken and my heart begins to race faster within my chest. I'm sure if I were connected to a heart monitor, my heart rate waves would have little love hearts flashing across the screen between each beat.

"Hey, Doc," Baylor flirts.

"Ms. Evans, I—"

"Please call me Bay." She flirts and again my blood simmers.

"Ms. Evans," he ignores her–score one Flynn. "As I was about to say, your X-ray shows no sign of a break, but the ligaments have been torn. You'll be in an orthopedic boot for a few weeks to aid in recovery of the ligaments, and you will need to follow up with a physical therapist to exercise and restrengthen the ligaments."

Baylor leans forward and thrusts for tits toward Flynn. "Can't you see me through my recovery?" she purrs like a desperado.

"No," he sternly says. "I'm an ER doctor, not a physical therapist. I'll have you fitted with a walking boot and then you'll be discharged." He turns to leave and looks at me. "Ave, don't forget to call me." With that statement he exits the cubicle, and I sit watching the curtain flap with a goofy grin on my face.

"What the fuck?" Bay scoffs. "He's choosing you over me?"

My grin evaporates at Bay's harsh words and I stare at her. "What?" I ask confused.

"Dr. Hottie totally ignored me and focused on you. Why?"

Shrugging my shoulders, I try to school my face because if Bay gets wind of my feelings—not that I have any—for Flynn then she'll swoop in and steal him like she did with Mike Ciz in eleventh grade. However, this time it will be much worse because I've already slept with Flynn, and there's something building inside me when it comes to the hot Irish doctor.

"Why?" she snarls again.

"Why not?" I bitchily say in reply.

"Because I'm me and you're you. You're a boring, quiet, shy school teacher. And I'm this…" She flicks her hand up and down her body. "Who wouldn't want this?"

Maybe it's your holier than thou attitude, I think to myself. "Bay, we look exactly the same except your hair is a little lighter, so on looks alone there's no comparison. Personality-wise…" I don't finish that because I don't want to get into an argument with her.

She rolls her eyes at me. "Whatever." She crosses her arms in a huff.

Thankfully a nurse walks in before it can get any more heated between the two of us. She gives Bay the details she needs for her physical therapist, fits her boot, and then hands her her discharge papers.

With the usual Bay overexaggeration, she climbs into the wheelchair and we leave the hospital. Just as we are exiting the ER, I feel Flynn staring at me from behind. Looking over my shoulder, I notice him watching me. He winks when our gaze meets and a smile breaks free. I brazenly wink back, something I wouldn't normally do, but around Flynn Kelly I seem to do a lot of things I normally wouldn't.

We arrive back at our apartment and Bay heads to her room, slamming the door behind her. Shaking my head, I walk into the kitchen and pour myself a glass of wine. With my wine in hand, I walk into the living room and as I take a seat on the sofa, I pull my phone out of my pocket.

Tucking my legs under my butt, I lean back into the sofa and grab the card Flynn gave me earlier. My nerves begin to jitter as I stare at the rectangular card in my hands. Pursing my lips, I umm and ahh as to whether I want to text him. I want to text him, really I do. But at the same time I don't. I totally don't know what to do right now. So instead of deciding, I chug back the wine in my glass. Hopping up, I refill it, and bring the bottle back with me.

Placing the bottle on the coffee table, I sit back down and take another sip. As the delicious crisp flavor of the pinot grigio hits my tongue, I decide to throw caution to the wind–a common trend when it comes to this man— and reach out to him. Adding his number to my phone, I stare at it before I whisper, "What the hell." And then I text him.

AVERY - *Hi, Flynn. It's Avery. If the offer still stands, I'd love to have dinner with you.*

That leaves the ball in his court and if he decides to ghost me, then I won't be too upset. Who am I kidding? I'll be gutted if he doesn't reply, but to my delight my phone beeps with a text a few minutes later. As I reach forward to pick it up, my heart rate accelerates with nerves. When I see his name on the screen, I grin like the Cheshire cat. Taking another sip of wine, I settle into the couch, unlock my phone, and read his reply.

FLYNN: *Hey, gorgeous. To be honest, I didn't think I'd hear from you. I thought I was going to have to resort to talking to your sister to get your number. Thanks for saving me from that. How about Friday night? I'll pick you up at 8.*

I smile at his reply.

>**AVERY:** *Friday sounds great. I'll meet you there.*
>**FLYNN:** *It's the gentlemanly thing to pick up his date.*
>**AVERY:** *This isn't the olden days. I'll meet you there, just tell me where.*
>**FLYNN:** *Let's meet at my place and we can go from there.*
>**FLYNN:** *You remember where that is, don't you?*

Smart-ass, I think to myself as I type my reply.

>**AVERY:** *Yes. See you Friday at 8.*

Placing my phone on the couch next to me, I shuffle back into the cushion and find myself smiling and then I sit up straight when it hits me. Holy shit, I'm going on a date with Dr. Kelly.

I'VE JUST FINISHED MY CRAZY, HECTIC, SUPER-SURPRISING extra shift and I'm exhausted. Grabbing my phone, I check for a message but there's no new messages. I'm not surprised, really. As I watched Avery leave the hospital earlier, it felt like it would be the last time I ever saw her. Honestly, I'm not holding out any hope of her texting me. After changing out of my scrubs, I grab my things and head to my car. As I'm climbing in, a text comes through, and much to my surprise and delight, it's from Avery. She DID text me, seems I was wrong in regards to her. Sitting in my car, I open her message with a goofy grin on my face and read. Normally I'd leave it and check/reply once I got home but knowing it's from her, I can't help myself.

Inwardly I do a little jig as I read her reply—yep, I'm

acting like teenage girl who has scored a date with the quarterback to the homecoming dance. Quickly I text back my dinner offer, and much to my delight, she replies immediately. She's either playing coy, or safe, not giving me her address but from what I know about her, she'll be playing it safe. She accepts my offer to meet at my place and with our date locked in for Friday, I throw my phone in the center console and head home.

I'm stopped at a red light and my mind drifts back to our night together. Her panting and screaming my name. The glazed-over look in her eyes when she comes. Man, I really hope we recreate and add to those memories on Friday. The honking of a car horn behind me snaps me back to the present. Looking up, I see the light is still green and I press my foot down on the accelerator and continue my drive home.

On the drive, my mind runs a million miles an hour with what we can do on Friday…and what I hope happens AFTER our dinner date. Whatever happens, I'm not going to let her slip through my fingers this time. I know I sound like a sap, but for the first time ever; I'm intrigued by a woman. I want to get to know Avery Evans. I want her in my life. I need to woo her and the wooing will start this coming Friday.

The week dragged by ever so slowly but finally, it's Friday. And just like the rest of the week, my shift passes by at a slow snail's pace. It's the slowest of slow days in the ER, and normally I'm all for a quiet shift but not today. I wanted today to fly by so I could get to tonight AND then I want for evening to go slow. *What the fuck is happening to me?* I'm A. Going on a date and B. I'm fucking excited for said date. Never in my thirty-three years have I ever been excited for a date; actually, I don't think I've ever been on a date date. Meeting in a bar to fuck isn't a date, it's a booty call with class. This is new territory for me. Do I get her flowers? Chocolates? A teddy bear? I don't know what to do and suddenly I'm nervous as all hell. What is this woman doing to me?

My shift is finally over and I hightail it out of the hospital. I brush off Preston when he asks about heading out for a drink. He eyes my suspiciously and I know that the next time I see him, he's going to grill me…but all going well, I'll have details to spill about a girlfriend. *What the fuck?* Where did that thought come from. Settle down, cowboy. Let's have our date before I start picking out china patterns. Thinking of that, my mind drifts to Avery in a white dress, standing before me on a beach. Her hair blowing in the wind. Shaking my head, I snap those crazy thoughts from my mind, pushing them deep down, and I head for home.

Stepping into my penthouse, I look around, and for the first time since moving in, it feels amiss. This place really needs a woman's touch and I think Avery is the woman to do that. Maybe after ravishing her all night long, I can ask her opinion in the morning…as long as she doesn't duck out on me again. That thought frightens the fuck out of me.

Avery Evans is invading my thoughts and changing my outlook on life. She's an enigma and I cannot wait for our date tonight to get to know her more.

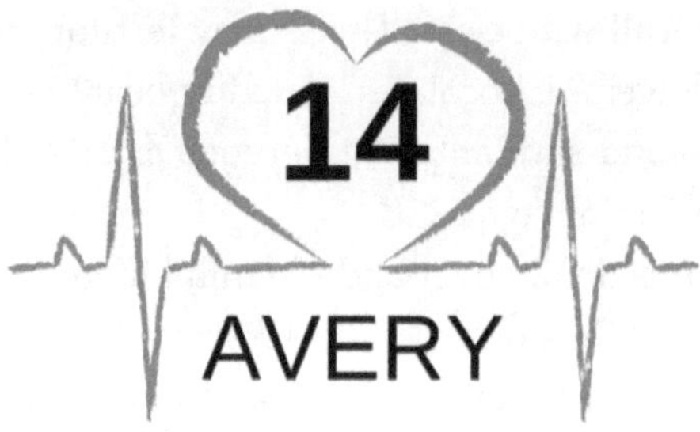

It's time to leave, I'm too nervous to drive so I order myself an Uber and it arrives quickly. The car pulls up in front of Flynn's building but I don't move. I sit here, staring at the back of the seat in front of me. Taking a deep breath, I step out and walk toward the entrance. The doorman opens the door for me and nods hello, but doesn't say anything. Smiling at the concierge, I walk toward the elevators, my heart excitedly racing with each step I take. Pressing the call button, the doors open and as I step in, my nerves kick in. I become a nervous ball of energy. My eyes watch the numbers as I travel up to the top floor. Nervously, I rub my hands up and down my dress a million times on the ride up. Biting my bottom lip, I let out a huge breath just as the elevator doors open. With a nervous sigh, I take a calming deep breath and step out into the penthouse foyer.

Holding my head up high, I walk toward his door. Raising my hand, I knock. Suddenly butterflies appear in my stomach and they begin to flap their wings rapidly. The door swings opens and when I see Flynn smiling back at me, all those nerves instantly disappear. "Hey," I greet. *Hey, really, Avery?*

"Hey," he says in reply. His eyes rake over me ever so slowly. His gaze setting my body on fire. "You look stunning, Avery." The deep timbre of his accented voice prickles my skin. Looking down at myself, I grin, *Yeah, this dress is smoking hot, thanks Cress for making me buy it.* And from the look on Flynn's face, I've knocked it out of the park tonight.

My eyes roam over him, and I too like what I see. I'm lost in everything that is Dr. Flynn ohh-so-sexy Kelly, and I can't believe I'm going out with him tonight. I feel like I've stepped into an alternate universe, hot guys don't fall me for. Bay? Yes. She's confident and outgoing. Me? I'm shy and reserved. My nerves ramp up again and doubt begins creeps in. I can't do this. I shouldn't be here. It isn't until Flynn touches my arm and smiles at me that everything settles down. The connection of his palm on me, instantly calms me. All those nerves evaporate and I feel like I can breathe again. We stare at one another. The air around us crackling with lust, desire, and everything in between.

"Evening, Dr. Kelly," I shyly offer, then I internally scold myself because I've already said hey. *Off to a swimming start here, Evans.*

"Evening, Ms. Evans," he says with a smile and wink.

My panties are now soaked. We continue to stare at one another and I'm ready to say screw dinner. I want to throw myself at the man before me and ravage him. Before my craziness comes to fruition, he steps into the hall and closes the door behind him. Stepping to me, he places a gentle kiss on my cheek and when he pulls back, my skin is tingling from the ever so brief kiss. Lifting my hand, I caress the spot where his lips just were and my smile widens. "Shall we?" he asks, offering me his elbow.

"We shall," I murmur, as I link my arm with his.

We spin around and make our way toward the elevator. We step into the car I just exited and as the doors close, the air around us electrifies once again. Standing next to one another, we not so subtly check the other out on the ride down. Flynn is rocking a pair of black slacks and a silver-gray button-down that accentuates his blue eyes, making them pop. His hair is styled in that sexy, messy man way and there's a slight five o'clock shadow gracing his chin.

The elevator arrives on the ground floor and we step out. He places his hand at my lower back and ushers me toward the exit. My heels click on the marble floor as we cross the lobby. The concierge nods toward us, and smiles. Flynn nods his head in return. "Evening, Max."

"Evening, Dr. Kelly." He pauses and looks to me. "Ms. Evans." Lifting my hand, I offer a shy wave and smile.

The doorman opens the door for us and when we step outside, I quiz Flynn, "How does he know my name?"

"I added you to the access list. That's how you got up without any concern earlier."

"Really? Why?"

"Because after tonight, I hope that you'll be visiting me often." *Whaaaat?*

He places a kiss on my temple and ushers me into a waiting car. I've been so wrapped up in this man that I didn't even notice the car idling at the curb. "Ohh, fancy. Do you always use a car service?"

"Not often, but I wanted to make tonight special."

Entering the car, I scoot across the seat and watch as Flynn climbs in beside me. I cannot help but ogle the sexy as sin man climbing in. How in the hell am I on a date with this man?

"Like what you see?" he cockily says, lifting his eyebrows teasingly.

"Meh." I shrug. "I've seen better," I playfully reply. *Wow, Avery, where is this sass coming from?*

"Really?" he counters.

"My lips are sealed." Mimicking locking my lips, I grin at him and wink. He smirks at me and a small laugh escapes me.

"I'm sure I can unseal them," he cockily replies.

He stares at me intently and then his gaze drops to my lips. My tongue darts out and I gently bite down. "I guess time will tell."

"Well then, looks like I need to up my game because, Avery, since I saw you at my door, I've really wanted to taste you again."

Swallowing deeply, I look to him seductively and whisper, "Why don't you then?"

"Because, if I kiss you now, I won't be able to stop, and I want to spoil you before I fuck you, plus, I wasn't referring to kissing the lips on your face."

My eyes bug open at the crassness of his statement but at the same time, my insides sizzle at the thought of what will come later. Sitting back in my seat, I stare out my window and grin. I really want him to kiss and ravish me. I want him to do everything to me.

Sneaking glances at the man beside me, my desire and

want builds with each mile the car travels along the freeway. "You know I can see you staring at me, right?"

My heads snaps to his. "How?"

"Because I'm staring at you, lass. I'm watching your every move. You, Avery Evans, are the sexiest woman alive, and I'm lucky as hell to be on a date with you this evening." He pauses and reaches over to take my hand in his. Lacing our fingers together, he rests our joined hands on his thigh. "When I saw you standing at my door, I was tempted to say screw the restaurant. I wanted to drag you inside where I'd feast on *you* for dinner, but then the sensible side of me kicked in and reluctantly but also happily, here we are."

Holy shit, he did not just say that to me.

Holy shit, we were thinking the same thing.

My mouth opens and closes a few times, words escape me and then my brain fires and words appear. "And I thank you for that, I'm starving."

"I am too…for you."

My eyes widen at his words and my panties dampen. Pursing my lips, I lower my gaze to my lap. My heart is racing right now, my insides are a buzz and my lady bits are throbbing. Biting my lower lip, I turn my head slightly and look directly into his eyes. "And for the record, Dr. Kelly, I would have totally been down with the ravishing of option one."

He shakes his head and laughs, a deep belly laugh that's music to my ears. "You continue to surprise me, Avery Evans."

"I continue to surprise myself too when I'm around you." Shuffling around, I face him. "Flynn, we are total opposites but there's something about you I'm drawn to. I couldn't stay away, even if I wanted to."

"Avery, I feel exactly the same way."

The rest of the car trip is silent but I do shuffle closer to him. Only a hair's width separating us, my hand traces circles on his knee, brazenly going higher and higher each time. Before I do something stupid, like straddle his lap and ravage him, we pull up to the restaurant. Flynn climbs out first, and offers me his hand.

As I step out, he says, "I hope you like steak." Looking up, I smile when I see we are at Rococo's Steakhouse, the finest steakhouse this side of Texas. We head toward the entrance, before he opens the door, I tug on his hand, stopping him. He turns to look to me. I smirk at him, leaning into him I whisper into his ear, "I love a big juicy piece of meat." Stepping back, I wink before I step past him and open the door to the restaurant.

He shakes his head at me and enters the restaurant behind me. We make our over to the maître d's station. "Good evening, welcome to Rococo's Steakhouse."

"Good evening. Reservation for Kelly."

"Welcome, Mr. Kelly. Your table is ready, if you'd like to follow me."

Flynn laces his fingers with mine and we follow the maître d' into the restaurant. I've never been here before and this place is gorgeous. When you enter there's rich wooden flooring that leads into the restaurant, where it changes to a deep plush burgundy carpet. The tables are dark in color, the chairs are a chocolate brown with studded accents and burgundy cushioning. Each table has a candle for ambience. The overhead lighting is dim but enough that you can still see. The kitchen it open and you can see inside. It's a hive of activity right now, pots clanging, steaks sizzling. The chef barking orders to the staff. Next to the kitchen is the bar which runs the length of the building. The front of the restaurant is floor-to-ceiling glass and the view of the city is spectacular.

Arriving at our table, Flynn pulls out my chair for me. "Thank you kind, sir."

He lowers down and whispers, "Don't thank me, I totally did that so I could see down your dress."

Playfully I smack his arm. "You fiend."

"Only for you," he replies, before he makes his way over to his chair. My eyes watch him. Even though he's tall and massive, he moves with the grace of a ballerina. He winks at me and I realize I'm in way over my head. Flynn Kelly is going to be the death of me…and I cannot wait.

Sitting across from Avery is hard...much like my dick right now. This woman is unbelievably sexy, and what makes her even more so, is the fact she is oblivious to how gorgeous she is. Right now, I want to be sitting next to her so I can caress and touch her. She smiles and it lights her face up, her eyes sparkle. It's in this moment I decide that sitting across from her isn't so bad after all. I can bask in her beauty and continue to check her out. Glancing around the restaurant, I look at everyone else, and no woman here compares to Avery. I just hope my cock decides to behave himself before I have to stand up.

"Flynn?" she yells, my eyes snap to hers. Her face is etched with concern.

Shaking my head to clear it, I question, "Sorry, what?"

"I asked, what do you recommend?"

With a grin, I saucily reply, "You…from memory."

Her cheeks tinge a sexy shade of pink. She bites her bottom lip. "I meant on the menu."

"Are you on the menu?" I tease.

She stares at me before leaning forward, giving me a stunning view down her dress. Her tits press together and I want the bury my face between them. They are looking mighty fine encased in satin, which so happens to match her dress, *I can't wait to see that bra on my floor*. She licks her lips before seductively whispering, "Maybe I can be your dessert later."

Cock.

Painfully.

Hard.

Again.

"You are a sexy little minx, Avery Evans. I'm totally holding you to that AND yes, for dessert I'm going to feast on you like I would a double chocolate fudge sundae. Every inch of you will be licked with my tongue and inspected with my fingers. When I've had my fill, I'll fuck you with my cock into the wee hours of the morning." He pauses. "I suggest you order the surf and turf…you are going to need your energy."

Her eyes pop open at my brashness and her cheeks darken my favorite shade of 'aroused pink.' She audibly gasps and swallows deeply. Her eyes become molten and I know she's thinking about what's coming after dinner. She goes to open her mouth in reply but the arrival of our waiter halts that conversation. She's flustered as she places her order, watching her squirm is quite entertaining. This woman continues to intrigue me.

As I watch her with the waiter, I grin to myself at how lucky I am to be here with this woman. I'm glad her sister hurt herself, as bad as that sounds, I mean it in the nicest possible way because it led me back to Avery and this time, I'm not letting her get away.

Dinner passes by quickly and smoothly, and thankfully, my cock has returned to normal. We laughed, lots, and the conversation flowed, as did the wine. There were no awkward silences. Avery and I get along surprisingly well, considering our vast differences. There is no more sexy talk but quite a few sexual innuendos are shared.

Every now and again, I'd feel her foot sliding up my calf; little minx that she is. The evening is easy and relaxed. It's utterly perfect. We finish the bottle of wine and the waiter appears. "Can I entice either of you with dessert?"

Avery's cheeks darken at the mention of dessert. I'm about to ask for the sticky toffee pudding when she beats me to the punch. "I think we're fine on the dessert front," she moves her gaze to me and adds, "you don't have what I would like on the menu." Again, she bites her lip and my cock begins to harden once again.

"Tea or coffee then?" the waiter asks, oblivious to the flirting and innuendoes floating around.

"Just the check, thanks," I answer.

"Certainly, sir." The waiter leaves and it's just the two of us again. The air is crackling right now. Avery lifts her hand and runs her fingers across her chest, up her neck before biting on her fingertip.

"Avery," I warn. "If you keep doing that, I'm going to throw you over this table and have my dessert right here."

"I'm down with that," she playfully replies.

"Minx," I say, as I pull my phone out and message the car service to pick us up. Once the message is sent, I look over to her. "Let's go." We stand up and make our way to the maître d'. Being a gentleman, I let her go before me. My eyes rake over her backside. "Fuck, that ass," I appreciatively whisper. It's obviously louder than I intended because she glances at me over her shoulder, winks, and then turns around, adding an extra sway to her hips. I settle the bill, to which she offers to go halves on. "No, I asked you out, therefore it's on me."

She nods but I can tell she's uncomfortable with that. She's the first woman to ever offer to pay after we've eaten, that gesture adds to her amazingness. She cups my cheek in her palm, her thumb gently caressing my jaw. "Thank you for dinner," she says, before kissing me on the cheek and turning to exit the restaurant.

The driver pulls up just as we exit. Holding the door open for her, we climb in and the driver pulls away from the curb. If I thought the air in the car on the trip here was thick and crackling, sitting in the back of the car now, it's stifling and getting hotter by the minute. I want nothing more than to pull her into my lap and take her now, but Avery deserves more than a backseat quickie and therefore I will be a gentleman and wait. But as soon as we get inside my penthouse, then it's all fair in orgasms and more orgasms.

Not liking the space between us, I reach over and rest my palm on her knee. Gently brushing my thumb back and forth. She squirms in her seat as my hand traces higher and higher. Just as we turn onto my street, I gently brush across her mound, a small illicit moan slips from her lips and it shoots straight to my cock. *Dammit, that backfired on me.* I cannot wait to hear her moan like that when she's naked and riding me. The driver pulls into the underground garage, it started to rain halfway home so I asked him to drop us off here so we don't get wet.

The driver stops by the elevators, I climb out and quickly walk around to open her door. Offering her my hand, she places her palm in mine and I help her out of the car. As we walk toward the elevators, she pulls on my hand. I immediately think she wants to go home. Turning to face her, I'm ready to plead my case as to why she should stay, but she shocks me by gripping my cheeks and pressing her lips to mine. Her tongue pushes inside my mouth and I willingly open. My hands slide into her hair and we devour each other's mouth. I've never much been a fan of kissing before but with Avery, I could quite happily kiss her for the rest of my life. "God, I missed your mouth. It's just as I remembered," I mumble, before I press my lips against hers again, fucking her mouth with my tongue. Reluctantly, I break the connection and rest my forehead on hers. We are both panting. "Shall we take this upstairs?"

She nods her head and grins. She places a quick kiss on my lips and reaches down to cup and squeeze my cock, my achingly hard cock, which is currently painfully pressing against my zipper. It's going to have teeth indents etched into the skin. She pulls away from me and steps over to the elevators and presses the call button. Standing in shock, I shake my head. This woman continually surprises me and if I'm not careful, Avery Evans will be the death of me...but what a fucking way to go.

Joining Avery by the elevator doors, we silently wait.

She reaches out to press the call button again and when she does, the doors immediately open. We climb in and I hit the 'P' for the penthouse. As soon as the doors close, the temperature instantly rises. Turning to face her, a force overtakes my body and I step to her. Walking her backward, I cage her against the sidewall with my body and grind my groin into her stomach. She moans and her sounds head straight to my balls.

Gripping her cheeks, much like she did to mine in the garage only moments ago, I slam my lips against hers. She drapes her arms around my shoulders and presses her body to mine. My arms lower and wrap around her waist as we continue to devour each other's mouth. "Ave lass, from this point forward, I want you to save all your kisses for me."

"Only if you save all your kisses for me."

"Deal."

Pressing my lips to hers again, I get back to kissing her. I can't wait to get her inside so I can kiss every inch of her delectable body. I will happily kiss no other person for the rest of my life, as long as I can continue to kiss Avery Evans. This woman has captivated me; heart, body, and soul.

The elevator doors open and with our lips fused together, I blindly step out and walk us toward my door. Without breaking the connection, I manage to open the door and step inside. She kicks it closed with her foot and as soon as the lock clicks, she removes herself from my arms. My face scrunches, as I don't like her not being in my embrace, but she shocks me—again— when she drops to her knees. She beckons me forward and I step to her. She reaches up, pops my fly open, lowers the zipper, and tugs my pants off my hips. Her eyes widen when she realizes I'm commando. Finally, I've shocked her but her surprise quickly morphs into hunger and desire.

Licking her lips, she smiles up at me. Her tongue darts out and she swirls it around the tip of my throbbing cock, precum coating her tongue. She massages my balls before taking me deep into her mouth. Puckering her cheeks, she gently sucks. My eyes drop closed and I lose myself to the sensation of my cock sliding in and out of her wet mouth. "Avery," I moan, as she continues to slide my cock in and out. Looking down at her, my cock hardens further at the sight of my cock sliding in between her delectable lips. She winks up at me and my balls begin to tingle. A sure sign I'm close. Reaching down, I pull her off me. "As much as I'm enjoying that, I do believe that YOU owe ME dessert." Seductively I raise my eyebrows but the little minx shocks me with her reply.

"Maybe I want my dessert first," I counter, before I lower my mouth back to his cock and resume sucking. Lifting my hand, I begin to stroke his cock in time with my sucking. He grips my head and guides it back and forth on his cock. His body becomes rigid and the first spray of hot salty cum hits the back of my throat. I continue to suck until he's finished.

Pulling back, I stare up at him. "MMMMM, my new fav dessert."

He shakes his head. "You, Avery Evans, are a constant surprise and a little minx. What am I going to do with you?"

Shrugging my shoulders, I stand up, and as I rise, I

grab the hem of my dress and lift it over my head. *Where has this bombshell version of me come from?* Dropping my dress to the floor, I'm standing before Flynn in nothing but my bra, panties, and heels. Taking a step back, I stare intently at him. My heart racing like never before. "I've always wanted to fuck wearing these heels." I lift my foot to the side to indicate my shoes. His gaze drops to them and then back up to me. My body heats at the intensity of his gaze. "And I want to be wearing these heels only," I pause for emphasis, "and I think tonight is the perfect time to make that wish come true." Reaching behind my back, I unsnap my bra and remove it. Letting it dangle from my fingertip, I drop it to the floor. It lands on top of my dress. I stare at Flynn, his eyes are full of hunger. Lust. Want. Desire. All of the above, and it's all for me. His breathing is ragged, much like mine. Even though he's just come, his dick is once again rock-hard and standing to attention. He steps out of this pants and stops just in front of me. Bending down, he throws me over his shoulder, I squeal in shock. With a slap to my ass, he turns around and heads toward his bedroom. Lowering me to my feet at the end of the bed, we stare at one another. He slides his fingers into the edge of my barely-there panties and tugs, the material snaps and disintegrates in his hands.

"Hey, I liked those," I complain, as he drops the material to the carpet.

"I'll buy you more," he growls, as he lowers to his knees in front of me. Pulling me to him, he presses his head to my mound and inhales. He places a kiss to my cleft and gently sucks. My head drops back on a moan when he flattens his tongue and slides it up and down my lips. "MMMMM," I moan. He squeezes my ass, bringing me closer to him. I grip the sides of his head and press him farther into me.

After a soul-crushing orgasm, just from his tongue, he gently pushes me back onto the bed. Lifting to rest on my elbows, I watch as he once again devours my pussy, just like he said he would at dinner tonight. Dropping to the mattress, I lose myself as my second orgasm of the night begins to build. This man is a freakin' god with his tongue. He builds me up and just when I think I'm going to crash over the edge, he pulls back and nuzzles my thigh, teasing me. Taunting me before diving back in again.

I can't take it anymore.

I need to come.

Gripping his head, I pull so he looks up at me. "If you don't let me come, I—" I don't get to finish that sentence because he thrusts two fingers inside of me, twisting them to hit that pleasure spot. My head drops back to the mattress. He continues to thrust his fingers in and out while simultaneously rubbing my clit. I've never felt plea-sure like this before. My body is buzzing. Thrumming with desire. He reaches up with his other hand and pinches my nipple. That action sets off a chain reaction of explosions. The most intense orgasm of my life detonates and explodes with such force that my body lifts off the mattress; I tremble from head to toe. My skin burns with desire. Falling back to the bed, I scream and moan as the pleasure continues to ripple through my body.

With one last kiss to my clit, my body comes back to Earth. I'm erratically breathing, like I've run a marathon. "Fuck me," I pant, trying to catch my breath and my body returns to normal.

"With pleasure," Flynn says as he stands up.

He removes his shirt, pulling it over his head in that sexy way guys do by grabbing the neck and lifting. He stands above me at the end of his bed, gloriously naked. His cock standing to attention and weeping. Spreading my legs, I lift my hand and with my finger I beckon him forward. He rests his knee on the end of the mattress and gazes down at me. "You look beautiful lying in my bed, but you know what will look even more stunning?"

"What's that?" I asks.

"Me fucking you on my bed."

"Well," I pause for effect. "What are you waiting for?" I boldly reply, as I slide my hand down my body and flick my clit. My body shudders at the sensation but it stops when Flynn rests his hand on mine.

"Ah uhh," he scoffs, "that's my job." He grabs a condom, sheaths his cock, and lowers himself between my legs. He lines his cock up with my entrance and with his eyes locked on mine, ever so slowly, he slides in. This intrusion is wonderful. Closing my eyes, I moan and enjoy the feeling of him filling me up. "Eyes on me, beautiful," he growls, as he begins to thrust his hips back and forth. Opening my eyes, I stare up at him. His muscles tense and flex as he thrusts in and out.

"Kiss me," I order.

He lowers himself down and kisses me. Wrapping my legs around his waist, I cross my ankles and the heels of my shoes dig into his ass. *This is better than I imagined*, I think to myself as our movements become frenzied. Our kisses hungry. Our teeth bumping as we thrust back and forth. My fingers dig into his shoulder blades, and I scream into our kiss as my orgasm appears out of nowhere and envelops me. My body quivers and as the remnants of orgasm number two, no three. Hell—I don't know—subsides, Flynn follows and he comes for the second time this evening.

Rolling off me, we stare at the ceiling. Both breathing heavily. "That was…"

I interrupt him, "Wow. Unfucking believable. Fantabulous. Out of this world amazing. Wow."

"You already said wow."

"It deserved two."

Rolling to my side, I rest my head in my palm and gaze at the man beside me. "Thank you," I murmur.

Rolling to face me, he rests his head in his palm like I am and smiles at me. "Why are you thanking me?"

"For tonight. I was hesitant to come on this date. I didn't want the amazingness of our first night to be replaced by an awkward dinner but…" I drift off, not sure if I want to voice this out loud.

"But what?" he questions.

"But I had nothing to worry about. From the moment I stepped out of the elevator, I was at ease. Being around you is easy. It's fun. You make me do things that I never do. You bring me to life in a different way. Hell, our first night together ticked off several of the 'never done before' boxes. I feel alive for the first time ever and I have you to thank for that."

"You are welcome and I agree. When I'm with you, everything seems easy. The world seems brighter. I'm so lucky to have met you, Avery Evans."

"I agree, Flynn Kelly. Thank you for bringing me to life."

"Thank you for letting me bring you to life."

We stare at one another, the air around us begins to crackle with desire once again. Leaning forward, I place my lips against his and before I know it, I'm riding him cowgirl style and another orgasm is crashing over me. After two or three more orgasms, hell I lost count after two, I blissfully fall asleep, naked and wrapped in Flynn's arms.

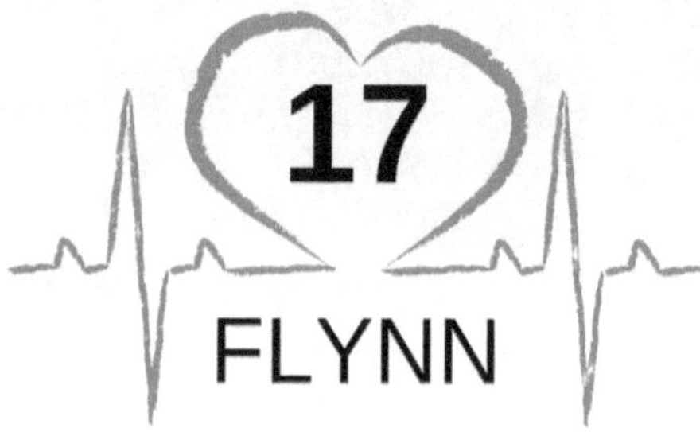

FLYNN

Opening my eyes, I look down and see her gorgeous hazel eyes locked on mine. She winks at me and proceeds to give me the best morning blow job of my life. Sooner than I would like to admit, I come with a guttural groan, spilling my seed down her throat. My cock pops out of her mouth; she wipes the corner of her lips, and seductively slips her finger into her mouth. "Morning," she whispers, as she slides in next to me. Draping her arm across my abs and tangling her legs with mine.

"Morning," I reply, brushing a tendril of hair behind her ear. "Sleep well?"

"Like the dead. You?"

"Best night sleep of my life AND the best way to wake

up. On our next sleepover, I would like to book a wake-up call like that."

"Duly noted." She leans up and presses her lips to mine. The moment is broken when a loud rumble comes from Avery.

"Hungry?" I ask, just as my stomach makes its own loud grumble.

"Seems we are both hungry…for food."

"Amongst other things," I say with a wink.

Rolling her to her back, I press her into the mattress and I slam my mouth over hers. Kissing the life out of her before fucking her. After a few more orgasms, we finally crawl out of bed and make it to the shower. There we add another few orgasms to the tally before finally washing each other. Stepping out we dry off, and I hand Avery a shirt of mine. She slips it over her head and I gaze at her. "I like you wearing my shirt."

"I like wearing your shirt."

Pulling on a pair of sweats, I step to her and wrap my arms around her waist. "I especially like the no panties option." Sliding my hand under the hem of the shirt, I grip her taut ass in my palm and squeeze.

"Well, if someone hadn't shredded mine, I'd have underwear to wear."

Shrugging at her, I grab her hand and start walking out of my bedroom. "I think I need to feed you now, you're getting hangry."

Avery rolls her eyes at me and follows me into the kitchen. She takes a seat at the island counter and I whip up breakfast for us. It's a simple meal consisting of coffee and fruit. "Sorry, it's not much. I didn't really plan for the morning after."

"It's fine, Flynn. I'm not a breakfast person anyway, coffee would have been fine."

Throughout breakfast we chat and laugh.

"You guys really swapped and no one knew?"

She nods her head. "Yeah, when we were little we got away with it easily but when we got older, our differences started to show. I remember one time in high school, I pretended to be Bay and took an exam, can't remember how we were caught, but Mom and Dad were so angry at us. We kinda stopped after that."

"I bet you were a cute kid."

"Says the cute one."

"I'm not cute," I retort.

"Yeah, you are and I bet you were a heartbreaker too. Leaving broken hearts behind in Ireland and at med school."

"I can neither confirm nor deny that accusation."

"I call bullshit."

Even though Ave and I are so different, we do have many similar interests: snowshoeing, wine, socializing, we each love dumb mind-numbing games on our phones. I realize, when I'm with her, it's comfortable. It feels like we've known each other for years and not just a few weeks.

"We should totally do that one weekend in the winter." Her words warm my heart; they don't freak me out. The fact she's thinking ahead and thinking about us still being together in a few months' time makes me smile, this isn't just some fling to her and that makes me ecstatically happy, because this isn't just some fling for me either. I want more with this amazing woman. I think I could fall for her…and I hope she could fall for me too.

"Why are you grinning like the Cheshire cat?"

"You just said we should go snowshoeing together."

"And?"

"Winter is months away. You're planning in the future for us."

"And?"

"And it surprised me."

"How so?" she questions, as she grabs our breakfast dishes and places them in the dishwasher.

"Well, after sneaking out and then your hesitance to go out with me, I didn't think you were interested."

She steps around the island and in between my thighs. She wraps her arms around my neck. "Flynn, you took me by surprise that first night, and yes, it really freaked me out, but when I saw you again, something changed within me. And last night was the best night of my life. Great dinner. Amazing company. Pretty good sex—"

"Only pretty good? I think the sex was more along the lines of fucking amazing. Best ever."

"Okay, your description of the sex is better than mine and one-hundred-percent accurate. But what I'm trying to articulate is that our connection isn't just physical. It's emotional too. I haven't felt inferior or awkward once with you. You bring me to life, Flynn, I've never felt like this before."

"Me neither, Ave." Her smiles widens. "Why are *you* now grinning like the Cheshire cat?"

"You called me Ave."

"So?"

"I normally hate being called Ave, but when you do, I kinda love it."

"Well, then, Ave lass, I want to know when we can do it again."

"Do what again?"

"Last night?"

"The date or sex?"

"Both," I nonchalantly say.

"Dinner next weekend." She pauses and bites her lip, then she lifts my shirt off her body and drops it to the tiles. "As for the sex, I say now."

She walks backward and when she hits the sofa, she lies down and beckons me forward with her finger. Standing up, I pull down my sweats and walk over to her. Stopping at the end of the sofa, I stare down at her. "Shit," I mumble.

"What?"

"The condoms are in the bedroom."

"I'm still on the pill and you are still the only person I've never used protection with before."

"Are you sure?"

She nods her head. "Yes, now fuck me, Flynn."

And fuck her I do.

We spend the rest of the morning fucking like rabbits, exploring every inch of each other's body. They say opposites attract and the attraction between Avery and me, it's explosive. I just hope we can survive the fallout if it comes to that.

FLYNN DROPS ME HOME MID-AFTERNOON. I HAVE TO SAY, LAST night was the best date of my life. Flynn is so different from what I thought and he brings me to life in a way like never before. The car ride home was quiet but not awkward. He pulls up in front of my building, leans across the center console, and kisses me. The kiss is searing hot and leaves me wanting more. I'm tempted to drag him upstairs and ravage him, but my nether regions ache and need a rest.

Standing on the curb, I watch him pull away. He's off to meet his friend, Preston, for an impromptu game of basketball, with a promise to call me later this evening. When his car is out of sight, I turn around and head up to the apartment. Unlocking the front door, I step inside and instantly I'm met with an irate Baylor. "Where the hell have you been?" she bellows at me before I've even closed the door.

"I told you, I had a date."

"You left yesterday evening. It's the afternoon on the following day. I needed you," she whines.

"I'm sorry, Bay. I thought you'd be okay for one night. I'm here now, what do you need?"

"It's fine now," she snaps. "I called a friend. She came running to help when she heard I'd been in the hospital."

"Seriously, Bay. You have a sprained ankle. You were in the ER for all of five hours. You are not dying and you can totally look after yourself. I think I can have one night out for a date."

"What if I'd fallen? What if I'd have died? You wouldn't have known for hours."

Dramatic much? I think to myself as I walk inside. "Quit with the drama, Bay. You're fine. You survived the night without me."

She rolls her eyes in typical overdramatic Bay style. She was always the drama queen when we were growing up. As much as we look alike, we are polar opposites personality-wise. "Who did you go out with?"

"Flynn."

"The hot doctor?" Nodding my head, I smile as memories of last night, and this morning, come flooding back to me but her next sentence cuts me to the bone. "Why would he go out with you?" she snarls, placing emphasis on the word you.

"Why not?" I defensively ask.

"It's you. Boring Ms. Evans, grade school teacher."

"Tell me how you really feel," I joke, but in what's

become Bay's new way of life, she lets loose but this time, there's vengeance and hurt behind her words.

"Okay, I will. You get everything handed to you on a friggin' silver platter. I try my hardest and I still struggle. You, are the sweet and innocent one. You always swoop in and make everything look easy and perfect. You're a new-age Mary-fucking-Poppins, and you make me sick. One of these days, you will fall off your pedestal and I will be the first person in line to laugh and laugh. Now if you don't mind, I need to rest my ankle that you don't seem to give a rat's ass about."

My mouth drops open at her response. She stands up and storms toward me, walking just fine on her ankle. She stops in front of me, breathing heavily. She sweetly smiles at me. "Don't get too comfy with your doctor."

"Why not?"

"There's no way you'll keep a stud muffin like him." She pokes me in the chest. "Dud and stud don't go together. This isn't one of those romance drivels you read. Avie, this is real life and no one gets a happily ever after." Her eyes glisten as she says this last part. "I'm going to my room to rest." She turns and walks away from me. Before she heads down the hall, she adds, "Clean up this place once you've pull your head out of your loved-up, skinny ass and remember what I said, it's not gonna last."

To say I'm shocked at what she just said to me is an understatement. I'm left standing in the living room, stunned and hurt by what just went down between the two of us. Baylor and I are different people, each to our own, but we've always been kind to one another. Just now, she was brutal and harsh; we've never been nasty like this before. She and I may be twins but apart from sharing a womb and kinda sorta looking like each other, right now, we share no other traits. She's become selfish and pushes the boundaries. Lately she expects everything to be done for her; which usually happens because she manipulates people, me included, to get her way or what she wants. She and I have become polar opposites on every level and even though she just tore me a new one, I still love her. Something is up with her at the moment but she won't let me in. She's being harsh and pushing me away to protect herself but I refuse to give up on her. She's my twinsie and I want the best for my sister. There is one thing though, I'm going to prove her wrong when it comes to Flynn. He and I will work out...I hope.

I've just climbed into bed and I'm shattered, today was tiring; emotionally and physically. My morning started out amazing, more than amazing and after ten minutes with Bay, it all went to shit. The only good thing to come from the angst filled afternoon; our apartment is now spotless. At least she can't gripe about that anymore.

From the moment I stepped through the door, nothing I did was right and she berated me at every chance. I would have preferred if she'd given me the cold shoulder, like she used to when we were little and she was in a mood. Actually, I wish she was like she was when we were little, I want my BayBay back.

My phone vibrates with a message. Picking it up, I smile when I see it's from Flynn.

FLYNN: *Nite, gorgeous. Just got to the hospital for my*

shift but wanted to touch base before I got started.
Miss you and can't wait to see you soon

A smile breaks free as I read his words. With one message he made all the shit disappear.

AVERY: *That was just what I need. Hope you have a great shift Xo*
FLYNN: *Why so glum?*

My fingers hover over the keyboard, I don't know if I want to bother him with my Bay issue, so I err on the side of caution with my reply.

AVERY: *Not glum. Just tired and missing you. Some fiend last night kept me up for hours and hours with multiple orgasms and a marathon sex session.*
FLYNN: *Sounds like a wonderful nite to me.*
FLYNN: *We should do it again.*
FLYNN: *Soon.*
AVERY: *That can be arranged. **wink***
FLYNN: *When and where? I'll be there. **wink wink***
AVERY: *Ummm….Let me cook you dinner Tuesday night.*
FLYNN: *What's for dessert? **wink wink wink***
AVERY: *Me **wink wink wink wink***
FLYNN: *We need to stop this. I'm sporting a major woodie right now and I have a 12-hour ER shift ahead of me. It's not off to a good start.*
AVERY: *It will be hard **pun intended** but you'll be fine. Nite Flynn*
FLYNN: *You are going to be the death of me, Avery Evans. Nite Ave lass*

With a smile on my face, I happily drift off to sleep and dream sexy things about Flynn and me. Waking early, I decide to head to Western General to surprise Flynn with breakfast. On my way to the hospital, I stop at *Starbucks* and grab two coffees and some pastries. Parking my car, I climb out and balance the pastries, coffees, and my handbag and head toward the ER. Someone yells out what I think was Baylor, looking around I can't see anyone so I keep walking, and then I hear that same voice yell, "Fine, be a bitch then." Looking around I still can't see anyone so I turn back around and keep walking.

Stepping inside, I look around, the waiting room is empty. As I'm looking around, the hairs on my neck stand on end and I feel Flynn before I see him. Looking up, he stops midstep when he sees me. His face is void of emotion and I begin to think I made a mistake in coming here, but then the biggest smile graces his gorgeous tired face. "Ave lass, what are you doing here?"

Hearing him call me Ave lass does things to me I've never felt before. I don't know whether it's his accent or just him, but whatever it is, my body comes alive being in his presence. As we walk toward each other, I find myself grinning and giddy with excitement. "Morning, Doctor," I purr, yes, I actually purr. "I thought you'd like coffee and pastries after a long HARD shift." Placing emphasis on the word hard, I smirk at him.

"I'm addicted to you, as much as you are addicted to the liquid in that cup you are holding."

"So not much then?" I playfully tease.

He shakes his head as he wraps one arm around my waist, pulling me into him. He places a kiss on my temple and my panties immediately dampen when his lips connect with my skin. A moan breaks free and when Flynn stares at me, he knows exactly what I'm feeling. "You, my little minx, are a devil." He lowers his voice and whispers, "I cannot wait to get you naked and fuck the sass out of you."

Winking, I quietly murmur, "You can try as much as you like—" The moment is interrupted when the doors to the ER slam open and a man frantically rushes in, a young boy in his arms.

"Help, I need help!" he screams.

Flynn immediately races over to the man and goes into doctor mode. I'm frozen on the spot. The once quiet ER is now swarming with the family of the child. A nurse arrives with a gurney and then Flynn and the nurse take the child from the man and place his tiny little body onto the bed and whisk him away, with his parents close on their heels.

I'm a quivering mess watching the scene before me play out. How Flynn does this on a daily basis is beyond me. Taking a seat in the ER, I decide to wait for him, since I don't have anything better to do on this Sunday morning.

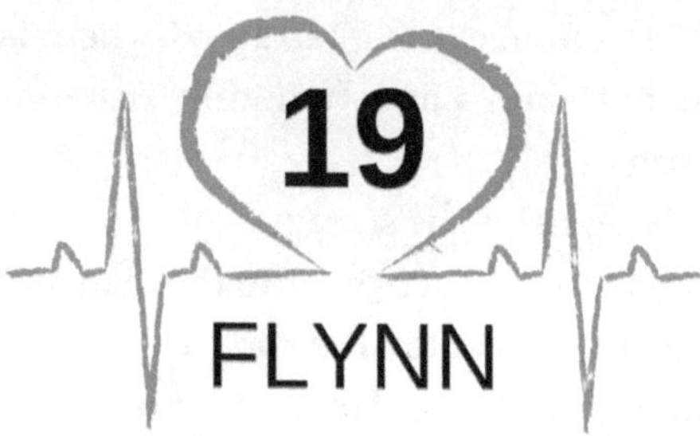

After handing the little boy and his care over to Preston, I let out a sigh. It's always tough dealing with kids, but today is a good day, as the kid will make a full recovery after a few days in hospital. Stepping back into the ER, a grin appears on my face when I look over and see Avery is still here. She's sitting in the corner and chatting with an elderly gentleman. From my spot I watch them, she looks happy and carefree. Just seeing her so joyous warms me from the inside. The gentleman says something and it causes her to laugh, a deep belly laugh. Her giggle filters through the waiting room like music.

She looks up and when her eyes lock with mine, she smiles at me and the grin that was already on my face increases. Walking over to them, I bend down and place a kiss on her head. "Avery, you're still here." My voice is laced with surprise, because I am. I didn't expect her to wait around for me.

She nods. "Yep, I had no other plans this morning so thought I'd hang around and wait. While waiting, I met Mr. Marshall here, and he helped me pass the time." Looking to the man, I nod.

"Marvin Marshall," he says offering me his hand.

"Flynn Kelly," I reply as I shake his hand, but before we can chat more, a nurse comes barrelling over to the three of us. "Marvin Marshall," she scolds, "we have been looking everywhere for you." She stops next to me and is glaring at Marvin.

"You said I couldn't go outside the hospital. Last time I checked, the ER waiting room was *inside* the hospital." He air quotes inside. Avery and I both laugh, until we see the look on the nurse's face.

"Dr. Kelly," she sternly says in greeting.

"Hi, Helen," I reply, "How are you?"

"Better now I found this one." She hooks her finger toward Marvin. "I swear the older they get, the worse they become."

"I heard that," Marvin says.

"You were meant to," Helen spits back at him.

Marvin leans over to Avery and not so quietly quips, "I think I'm in trouble but to spend the morning with a gorgeous girl like you, it's totally worth it." He winks at her before he turns his attention to me. "Look after this one," nodding his head toward Avery, he states, "she's a keeper."

"I think you're right, Marvin," I reply, my gaze on Avery's as I say this. Her cheeks tinge that lovely shade of pink I love seeing on her.

"We need to get you back to your room, Marvin," Helen says.

Avery stands up first and offers her hand to Marvin. With a bit of a struggle, he stands up and steps toward Helen. Avery reaches out to stop him. She squeezes his arm and when he turns to face her, she leans down and places a goodbye kiss on his cheek. His face lights up like a Christmas tree and I think this morning is the highlight of his year. "Goodbye, Marvin."

"Bye, Avery." Marvin and Helen walk away. Helen walking slowly to aid a shuffling Marvin. Marvin mumbles something that garners him an evil-eyed stare from Helen. Both Avery and I laugh as we watch them exit the ER.

Stepping to Avery, I brush a tendril of hair behind her ear. "You really are something, Avery Evans."

"A good something, I hope," she shyly replies.

"A very good something." Leaning down, I place my lips against hers for a quick kiss. It turns heated and not really appropriate for the ER, but I don't care. If I want to kiss Avery, I'll kiss Avery no matter the location. Pulling back, I rest my forehead on hers. "Give me ten to change, then I can meet you at my place?"

She nods her head. "I like that plan."

Kissing the tip of her nose, I turn and go change. Ten minutes later, I've changed and I'm racing to my car. Traffic is light this morning, surprisingly, and I make it home in good time. When I arrive, I park in my spot and rather than wait for the elevator, I take the stairs, two at a time, and make my way up to the lobby to meet Avery.

Stepping out, I smile when I see Avery waiting for me. She's leaning against the front desk, chatting with Max.

"Good morning, Dr. Kelly," Max says when he sees me.

"Morning, Max." Turning my attention to Avery, I ask, "You ready?"

"Yep." She turns to Max and says, "Have a great day, Max."

"You too, Ms. Evans."

"Please, call me Avery." He nods at her and she picks up a tray of coffees and we walk toward the elevators. Lacing my fingers with hers, we fall into step with one another as we head toward the elevators. The doors open and a delivery guy exits, we step in and I press the button for the penthouse.

"Hope you don't mind, I stopped and got coffee for me and a tea for you on the way here."

"Not at all, I'm just happy to have you here, the hot drinks are just a bonus."

"I won't stay long as I know you need to sleep."

"I'd love to sleep with you." She eyes me. "Not like that, you fiend, in the literal close your eyes sleep sense BUT if that was to happen, I wouldn't complain." I pause and then add, "I love waking up with you in my arms."

"Well, since I got a full night's sleep. How about I lie with you while you drift off and then I'll come back later this afternoon?"

"OR you can just spend the day at my place so you are here when I wake up?"

"Really?" she asks and I nod in reply, "Okay, sure, why not. Just for you, I'll spend the day lazing around in a gorgeous penthouse."

"Perfect." Leaning down, I press a kiss to her temple and breath her in.

We are quiet for the rest of the trip. Entering the penthouse, Avery heads to the living room and sits on the sofa. Taking a seat next to her, she hands me my tea. We drink them in silence. Once finished, Avery tidies up and I grab a quick shower since I didn't have one before leaving the hospital. When I step out of the en suite I smile when I see Avery is in my bed. She's slipped into one of my shirts, and can I say, I love seeing her in my clothes. She's reading on her iPad. She looks up and the vision before me is indescribable.

Grinning down at her, I walk around the bed in nothing but my towel, when I reach my side, I drop the towel to the floor and stand there. Her gaze drops from my face and is now locked on my cock. I stand beside the bed and stare at her. She looks up at me, her cheeks once again pink, and with a wink, I pull back the covers and climb in next to her.

Draping my arm across her stomach, I snuggle into her side as she sits in bed and continues to read. She begins massaging my scalp and soon slumber overtakes me. I fall into a deep blissful sleep, snuggled into Avery.

It's mid-afternoon when I wake again. Reaching out, my hand meets a cold sheet, Avery isn't in bed and a wave of sadness washes over me. I really thought she'd stay and then I hear noise coming from the living room. Slipping on a pair of sweats, I follow the sound and stop midstep. From my spot in the hallway, I watch Avery. She's in her own little world, singing along to "Wolves" by Selena Gomez playing from her iPod, which she's connected to my speaker system.

Leaning against the wall, I cross my arms and watch as she swings her hips and wipes down the kitchen counter, oblivious to me watching her. The song changes to "Havana" by Camila Cabello and she seductively sways her hips from side to side. My cock twitches at the sight of her ass swishing from side to side. She's still wearing my shirt and I find myself grinning at the sight before me. Taking a deep breath, my smile increases when the most amazing, sweetest scent ever to come from my kitchen envelops me. That's when I notice a tray of decadent-looking iced cupcakes sitting on the counter, waiting for me eat.

She finally notices me and jumps in fright. She squeals, and brings her hand to her chest.

"Sorry, didn't mean to scare you."

"It's okay, I hope I didn't wake you, when I bake I listen to music and sing. I guess I got a little carried away." She turns to the sink and rinses the cloth.

Walking over to her, I shake my head, "No, you didn't wake me." When I reach her, I wrap my arms around her from behind and place a kiss on her shoulder. "Morning."

"Afternoon," she says, turning her head, allowing me to place a kiss on her lips.

"You taste like frosting," I huskily murmur.

She licks her lips. "Had to taste test and make sure it had the right amount of vanilla."

"Is that so?" I ask, as she spins in my arms and drapes hers over my shoulders.

"Yep," she says. Lifting her up, I carry her and place her onto the island countertop. She spreads her legs and I step between them as we gaze into each other's eyes. Without breaking eye contact, I reach behind her and grab a cupcake. Glancing at the decadent-looking masterpiece in my hands, I inspect it as if I'm a judge on *Cake Wars*. "It looks pretty great to me, but I better taste one just to be sure."

She takes the cupcake from me and peels back the muffin paper and offers it to me. Opening my mouth, I take a bite and instantly moan. My mouth is assaulted with the delicious combination of vanilla icing and light fluffy chocolate sponge. Offering the cake to her, she leans forward and takes a bite.

"MMMMM," she moans, lifting her gaze to mine.

My eyes drop to her lips, her tongue darts out, and she gently bites her lip. *Dick, instantly hard.* Noticing a smidge of frosting at the corner of her mouth, I lean forward and lick before pressing my lips to hers for a kiss. Sliding my tongue into her mouth, I wrap my arms around her waist, pulling her into me and deepening the kiss. Our tongues slide around each other's mouth, and my hands wander up and down her back before sliding around the front to cup her boobs in my hand. Gently I squeeze her plump mounds that fit perfectly into the palm of my hand. Gently I push her back onto the counter, sliding my hand precariously slowly down her chest. Leaning over her, I lower my head and suck one of her nipples through my shirt. She moans beneath me. Her back arches. Kissing my way down her stomach, I lift her—my—shirt and circle my tongue around her belly button.

"Please," she whimpers, as she runs her fingers through my hair. Her nails scratching at my scalp.

Placing featherlight kisses along her stomach, I kiss down toward her panties. Today she's wearing plain pink cotton and I see a wet patch between her thighs. Grazing my nose up and down her material-covered slit, she moans and thrusts herself upward. Pushing on her stomach to hold her down, I suck and kiss her through the material covering her.

"Please," she whines, tugging on my hair.

Lifting my gaze, and standing up, I stare down at her. She looks utterly divine laid out on my island counter. Reaching down, I grab the sides of her panties and tug them down her legs. Dropping them to the tiled floor, I look back at my girl. She spreads her legs wide open, resting her heels on the edge of the countertop. Giving me an uninterrupted view of her pussy, her lips shining with her arousal and her clit peeking out.

"Please, Flynn," she begs and this time I don't deny her. I lower my head between her thighs and I devour her with my tongue and fingers like a starved man. If I died right now, I would die a happy man.

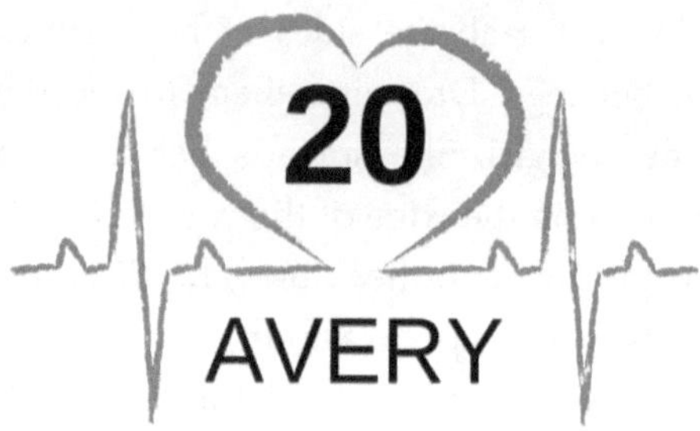

FINALLY, HE GIVES ME WHAT I NEED. HIS HEAD BETWEEN MY thighs. His tongue sliding up and down my folds. His thumb pressing on my clit. A guttural moan slips from my lips when at long last, he slips a finger inside me. "Yes. Yes. Yes," I mewl. He slides two or three, I'm not sure how many, more into me. My body hums with arousal, I never want this feeling to subside. *If I died right now, I would die a happy woman*, I think to myself as I lift my hands to my breasts and massage them through Flynn's shirt. Pinching my nipples between my thumb and forefinger, I play with my breasts while Flynn plays with my pussy. Finally, my orgasm erupts and I scream. My back arches. My body clenches tight. My thighs press together, trapping Flynn between my legs. I soak Flynn's face with my juices as pleasure rockets through my body.

Loosening their vise-like grip on Flynn's head, he lifts from between my thighs, his chin and lips shiny with my arousal. He licks his lips. "Mmmm."

Sitting up, I lift his shirt over my head and scoot toward the edge of the counter. Sliding my hands into his sweats, I push them down and his cock springs free. He steps out of his pants and I reach forward and grip his erection in my hands. Giving it a few strokes before I guide it between my thighs. Lining it up at my entrance, I look up at him and whisper, "Fuck me, Flynn."

We both thrust forward and I impale myself on him. A moan slips free as our hips rock back and forth. Sliding his hand under my ass, he lifts me up and I wrap my legs around his waist. He spins around and presses my back into the wall as he continues to thrust himself in and out. His lips devour mine. He kisses his way down my neck until he's at my breasts, taking a nipple into his mouth, he sucks before gently biting the tip.

"Flynn!" I shout. "I'm close," I mumble.

Lifting his head from my breast, he stares into my eyes and continues to piston himself in and out of me. "Let go, lass."

With his words, I let go and tumble over the orgasmic edge. My walls clench around his cock. My fingers dig into his shoulders and I ride out my second release of the afternoon. My body is still buzzing when I feel him tense against me and with a gravelly grunt, he too comes. Resting my forehead against his, he empties himself inside me. Pulling away as he finishes, he stares at me, panting deeply.

He rests his forehead against mine again as we each settle our breathing. My eyes drift closed and I run my fingers absentmindedly through his hair. With my eyes still closed, I feel my body moving. I feel like I'm flying. Opening my eyes, I see Flynn is walking us into his en suite. He places me on the vanity and I watch as he spins around and leans into the shower, turning the water on. He closes the glass door and the cubicle begins to fill with steam.

Spinning back, he steps toward me and places a kiss on the tip of my nose. He reaches down and lifts me into his arms, hugging me to him. Instinctively, my legs wrap around his hips and I hold onto him like a monkey.

"You do know, I have these things called legs and I can walk?"

"Ohh I know you have killer, sexy as fuck legs, Avery, I just like having you in my arms."

SWOON, ovaries exploding, this man seriously is going to be the death of me.

"I like being in your arms too, and you also have pretty amazing legs and a sexy ass." Lifting my head from its resting place on his chest, I kiss and nibble his jaw. His scruff tickling my lips. Pressing my lips to his, I kiss him, my tongue licking along the seam before sliding into his mouth. He stops walking toward the shower and deepens our kiss.

Pulling free, we stare at one another. Our lips plump and bruised from our kiss. With a wink, he walks toward the shower and opens the door. Stepping in, the hot water hits my skin and I moan. The pressure and heat feels amazing. Dropping my head back, I close my eyes and let the water cascade down my face and body.

Flynn lowers me to my feet and spins me around. Running his hand up my side, he begins to massage my shoulders. A pleasurable moan erupts in the back of my throat. Dropping my head forward, I completely relax. The combination of the warm water and his fingers digging into my muscles is pure bliss. A contented relaxed sigh breaks free, I'm seriously in heaven right now.

"Avery, if you keep moaning like that, I will not be held accountable for what I do to you in here."

"Mmmhmpf," I reply.

Leaning forward, I rest my forehead against the tiled wall and enjoy the massage he's currently giving me. Flynn cocoons me in, the warmth from his body adds to my chilled-out state. His cock is pressing against my ass. Circling my hip, his cock hardens between us. Reaching behind me, I grip his girth in my palm and begin to stroke. He squeezes and massages my shoulders and I squeeze and massage his cock. Turning to face him, I wink before dropping to my knees. Licking my lips, I open wide and take his cock deep into my mouth. Sliding it out, I suck the tip, swirling my tongue around before sucking back down again. Repeating this over and over. Flynn moans from above and slides his hands into my hair. He guides my head up and down his shaft. Cupping his balls, I gently massage them. Flynn hisses and then I feel them tighten in my hand. With a guttural growl, he comes. I suck every last drop of salty cum down my throat. Sitting back on my heels, I gaze up at him, and I realize in this moment, I am falling for Flynn Kelly and I could quite easily fall in love with him. I get the urge to tell him, I want to tell him.

Standing up, I take his hands in mine and just as I'm about to tell him, his beeper beeps, breaking the spell on the moment.

"That'll be the hospital, I need to get that." Nodding

my head, he steps out. Looking back he adds, "Be right back, don't go anywhere."

"There's nowhere else I want to be," I whisper as I watch him.

Taking the opportunity, I pump some bodywash onto my hands and begin to wash myself. I feel him before I see him, spinning around he looks sad. "What's wrong?"

"I need to go into work early. I know we were going to have dinner—"

"Don't apologize, we can do dinner another time."

"You really are amazing, Avery Evans."

"I know," I confidently reply. "I'm finished, you hop in and I'll make you a coffee to go."

"Thank you," he says, his voice saddened by having to leave. Stepping out, he grabs a fluffy white towel and opens it for me. He wraps it around my body, enveloping me in. He holds me closely to him. Resting my head on his chest, the thrum of his heartbeat relaxes me. Squeezing my arms, I look up at him. He really is sexy; looks, personality, he's the perfect complete package. He places a kiss on my nose and hops back into the shower.

Stepping into his room, I redress in my clothes from earlier and head to the kitchen. I go about making his coffee and I clean up our cupcake mess. I've just finished wiping down the counter when Flynn walks out. Our gaze locks across the room. Neither one of us says anything. I'm just about to say those three words when my phone rings, glancing down I see it's Bay. Sending the call to voicemail, I ignore her. I'll call her back after I say goodbye to Flynn. I look up and see he's slipping his coat on. I realize the moment to tell him has now passed. It's probably a good thing, it's too soon to be feeling this. We've only known each other for a short time but when I'm with him, I feel different.

Picking up his coffee, I walk toward him and pass it to him. Slipping on my coat, we exit his apartment and hop into the elevator. He gets off at the lobby and walks me out to my car. After a NSFP—not suitable for public—kiss, I climb into my car and leave Flynn standing on the sidewalk. He watches as I drive off and with a smile on my face, I head home.

WALKING AWAY FROM AVERY JUST NOW IS THE HARDEST thing I have ever done. In a few short weeks, this woman has taken up residence in my heart and for the first time ever, I think I'm falling in love. To reiterate that point, "Can't Help Falling in Love" by Elvis begins to play. If that's not a sign—not that I believe in that shit—then I don't know what is.

Walking into the hospital, a melancholic feeling washes over me, but it quickly passes when a multi-vehicle accident occurs. The ER is swarming with people and I don't have time to think. It's the wee hours of the morning when Helen comes wandering into the ER, a scowl on her face. "Hi, Helen," one of the triage nurses says.

"Hey."

"To what do we owe the pleasure, Helen?" I ask.

"Marvin in missing again."

A laugh breaks free but I quickly stop when I see the murderous look on her face. "Want some help looking for our resident Houdini?"

"Please," she says, "This shit is getting old, he's worse than the kids in the children's ward."

"Well, they do say that's life's cycle. Baby. Child. Adult. Child. Death."

"That's a pretty morbid way to think of life," she replies.

"It's true though, when you look at it."

Stepping into the ER waiting room, I look around and sure enough, Marvin is in the corner chatting/flirting with a group of young girls. "Found him," I say, nudging Helen in the arm. She shakes her head and storms over to him.

"Marvin Marshall," she scolds, and from my spot next to her even I flinch, not Marvin though. He enrages the beast that is Nurse Helen and turns to his new friends. "Ohh oh, I'm in trouble."

The girls all giggle. He says goodbye to his friends and follows a still fuming Helen back toward his ward and room. "Dr. Kelly," Helen says as they walk past.

Marvin mimics Helen, "Dr. Kelly," garnering another evil glance from Helen.

Shaking my head, I walk back into the ER and decide to tackle the paperwork I have been putting off. With my arms laden with charts, I head toward the doctors' lounge. Dropping off the paperwork, I head across to the coffee shop and grab myself a coffee—the coffee in the cafeteria here tastes like shit. With my coffee in hand, I head back and get into the paperwork.

Before I know it, the sun is shining and it's morning.

My shift will be over in a few minutes and I want to see Avery. I decide that today, I will be the one to surprise her. Grabbing a quick shower, I change into denim jeans and a green Henley. Saying hi/bye to the doctors in the lounge, I race to my car and drive over to Avery's.

Traffic is a shitshow this morning and it takes me forever to get to her place. I'm agitated and antsy when I pull up out the front. Taking a few calming breaths, I cool down and climb out of my car. Looking at my watch, I hope she's awake, I don't want to wake her, but if she does happen to be sleeping, I'll just climb into bed with her. Either way it's a win/win.

Stopping at her door, I raise my hand and knock. The door opens and I'm pleasantly surprised when I see what she's wearing, then movement over her shoulder catches my eye and I realize it's Baylor at the door. She flirts but I ignore her advances, my eyes are locked on Avery's. She is unbelievably sexy this morning. Like me she is wearing denim jeans and hers hug her curves in that sexy as fuck way. She's wearing a black tank that accentuates her tiny hips and shows off the perfect amount of cleavage. "I'm here to pick up your gorgeous sister."

When I say this, Avery's face lights up. We say our goodbyes to Baylor and I escort my girlfriend to my car. On the way over, I planned a spur of the moment date. Sleep can wait, today is all about Avery Evans.

HIS EYES RAKE OVER HER BODY AND MY BLOOD BOILS. I SHAKE my head and roll my eyes and then his eyes find mine and his grin morphs into a megawatt smile that lights up his face; and mine. Ignoring Bay and her shameless flirting, he says, "I'm here to pick up your gorgeous sister."

"Awww, are you admitting I'm gorgeous?" He looks at Bay and scrunches his eyes in confusion. "You just said my sister is gorgeous. I'm her twin, therefore you think I'm gorgeous too, since we are two in the same."

She thrusts her tits toward him but his eyes are locked on me. Ignoring her he says, "You may be her twin, but I only have eyes for Avery." He steps around Bay and stalks over to me. "I only want her." Wrapping his arms around my waist, he pulls me into him, and kisses my cheek hello.

"What are you doing here?" I ask, as I stare up at him.

"We have a breakfast date," he matter-of-factly says, before he gently places his lips against mine for a sexy hello kiss that leaves me breathless. He pulls away and brushes a tendril of hair behind my ear. "Morning, beautiful."

"Morning," I manage to squeak out 'cause I'm kinda stunned right now. "I didn't realize we were doing breakfast this morning."

"Surprise!" he says, tapping the tip of my nose. "Ready to go?"

Nodding my head, I see from the corner of my eye Bay is still standing in the doorway. She's shooting daggers my way, she's pissed at being passed over by Flynn; again. "Sure. Let me grab my purse and we can go."

Grabbing my things, I link my fingers with his and we walk toward the door and Bay, who is still standing there. "Have a good day," I say to Bay as we pass. We step through the door into the hallway. Bay slams the door behind us, the frame rattling from the force, and through the wood I hear her mumbling profanities, presumably toward me. That seems to be the only way she talks to me at the moment. I can't do anything right when it comes to her right now. Something is definitely up with my twin, and normally we'd talk to one another about our worries and bounce ideas around to fix the problem. But for the last few weeks, even longer, she's been pulling away and changing before my eyes.

Flynn squeezes my hand and I can't help but smirk, for once a guy wants me and not her. I know it's petty to feel like this but I'm happy to win for once; score one for me. I play over the scene when he arrived in my head and my grin widens. Flynn ignored her advances and when he saw me, I became his sole focus. It was all about me and it felt pretty good to be the center of attention. I'm so happy right now, it's not often I get one up on her, and Flynn just helped me achieve that.

Looking over at him, I squeeze his hand back. "Thank you for that."

"Thanks for what?" he questions, his forehead scrunched in confusion.

"For ignoring her skanky, ho slutty, see-through nightie." I pause, then add, "For being you."

"Ave lass, I didn't even see what she was wearing. Well, I did, don't get me wrong." I eyeball him but he is correct, he is a man after all, and they don't always think with the right head. "I was surprised you'd wear something like that, but then you moved and my gaze gravitated over to you and from that moment, you were all I saw. Ave, when you are around, it's you and only you I see. No one else enters my mind."

My mouth drops open at his frank confession. "I feel exactly the same way when I'm around you. More often than not, I feel you before I see you." He nods in agreement. "Now, let's go eat. I'm starving."

"Well, I need to get you fuelled up because after breakfast, you are going to need lots of energy for what I have in mind."

At his words, my clit begins to throb between my thighs and suddenly I'm not hungry for food. Flynn whisks me to Maggie's, a small mom-and-pop diner just around the corner from my place. We each order pancakes, bacon, and coffee. After an amazing breakfast, we leave and I think we'll be heading back to Flynn's for some naked between the sheets fun, but he surprises me; again. Rather than heading back to his place, he heads to the The

Morton Arboretum and drags me toward the Maze Garden. It's an amazing one-acre, living hedge maze, and the maze changes with each season. "Ohh my God, Flynn, this place is amazing, I haven't been here in forever The last time I was here was with Cress for Lexi's fourth birthday."

"I've never been. I've been past here many times and this morning I thought, today is the day. I'm happy to pop my maze cherry with you."

"And I'm happy to pop your cherry." Taking his hand in mine, we head toward the entrance. Flynn and I spend hours chasing each other through the maze. We get lost many times but we have an absolute blast together. We manage to find all seven of the plant rooms, something I've never done before. I cannot remember the last time I laughed this much. We finally make our way out of the maze; I was starting to think we'd be trapped in there forever. I'm sweating like a pig and I feel gross. We head into the Ginkgo Restaurant and Cafe and I take the water the he offers me. Twisting off the cap, I take a mouthful. "That was so much fun. Not what I thought would be happening today."

"What did you think I had planned for today?"

My cheeks darken and I lower my head. Flynn places his finger under my chin. "What did you think, Ave?"

"I…ummm…ahh…I thought you were going to take me back to your place and you know—"

"You know what?" From the predatory look on his face, he knows exactly what I'm referring to.

"I thought we'd be naked and doing stuff, other fun stuff."

"Why you, little minx you." He places a kiss on the tip of my nose and gazes at me. He leans down and whispers,

"Let's get out of here and then we can definitely do that." He nibbles my earlobe, gently sucking.

Swallowing deeply, my body quivers when I think about what's going to happen as soon as we get back to his place. Then I remember I'm all sweaty and dirty and feel yucky. "Can I shower first? I'm all dirty and sweaty."

"Lass, you will be even dirtier and sweatier when I'm done with you, but I guess we can always start in the shower and see where we end up from there."

"I like the way you think, Dr. Kelly. Let's go," I say.

We head back to Flynn's and he makes good on his promise to get me even more sweaty and dirty. Flynn ravishes my body from head to toe, repeatedly.

All

Afternoon

Long…and well into the evening.

After our amazing sex-filled afternoon and evening, life as I knew it at the hospital became hectic. It feels like I live there at the moment and I haven't seen Avery in days. I'm missing her like crazy, which surprises me. I've never missed anyone before and people can tell that something's up. I'm grouchy with the staff. I'm not myself. I know I'm being a total asshole, but I can't help it. I miss Avery. And to top it off, on Wednesday something weird happened. I was walking in for my evening shift and I bumped into Baylor. I knew it was her from the way she was dressed— short, short Daisy Dukes and a pink top, if you could call it a top, as it left nothing to the imagination. She was heading out after her a physical therapy appointment and as usual, she flirted up a storm with me. And like always, I brushed her off but she was definitely different today. She was more forceful than usual and she even tried to pass herself off as Avery at the beginning, but the walking boot clearly gave her away. Orthopedic boot aside, I'm pretty sure I know the difference between my girlfriend and her twin. She's pretty persistent, that's for sure. That girl just won't take a hint but what frustrates me the most, is that she's doing this to her own sister. *Who does that?* We are interrupted by a sketchy-looking guy; he grabs Bay by the arm and drags her away. She smiles at me as he pulls her away but it doesn't feel sincere. I'm not sure if she's going willingly but that thought changes when she catches me staring at her. Lifting her hand to her lips, she blows me a kiss, and then turns her attention back to the guy she met up with and begins flirting with him. That chick clearly has issues, how she's related to Ave is beyond me. They are polar opposites…just like us really.

Shaking off the encounter, I head into the doctors' lounge to get ready for my shift. I've just pulled on my scrubs when my phone rings, glancing down I see Avery's smiling face on the screen. Picking it up, I answer immediately, "Ave lass, how are you?"

"I'm great. I just received the most gorgeous bunch of reddish-pink roses. You wouldn't know anything about that, would you?"

"Maybe."

"Seriously, Flynn, they are gorgeous. Thank you so much."

"You're welcome, lass. I've missed seeing you this week, but I wanted you to know that I'm thinking of you."

"Flynn, it's been three days."

"That's forever in Avery time."

"Aww, are you missing me, baby?" she teases, but she's correct. I am a lovesick fool missing his girlfriend, and I'm man enough to admit it, well to myself that is.

"Hell yes, I am. Any chance you can swing by the hospital later?"

"I was there earlier visiting Marvin." *Dammit, I missed her.* I pout, yes, I pout…thankful no one is around to see me acting like a pansy.

"How is our resident escapee?"

She swallows deeply. "Not doing too good. I'm worried about him." Her voice is laced with sorrow and sadness.

"What's wrong?" I ask, as I sit in front of my locker.

"He wasn't as spirited as usual." She sniffles, "I think he's going to die, Flynn."

"Ave lass, I'm so sorry." Wishing right now I could take her into my arms and give her the comfort that she needs. "If you like, I can check on him in the morning, and send you an update before you go to work."

"You'd do that for me?"

"I'll do anything for you, Avery."

"Thank you, Flynn, I'd really appreciate that. Thank you."

"Anything for you, Avery." We both go silent but it's not awkward or uncomfortable. "Sorry to cut this short, but my shift is about to start."

"No need to apologize, it's fine, now get to work and go save some lives."

"Will do. I'll call you in the morning with an update on Marvin."

"Thank you."

"Night, Avery."

"Night, Flynn."

Hanging up, I smile when I realize I've fallen head over heels for Avery Evans. I've never felt like this about a woman before. It's new territory for me, and I'm scared to death I'm going to fuck it up, but at the same time, I'm excited for the adventure ahead.

Finally my super busy nightshift is over. I'd love to just head home and crash, but I promised Avery I'd check in on Marvin. So here I am, in the elevator on my way up to his floor. When I walk into his room, I freeze midstep when my eyes land on him in his bed. He really has deteriorated since I last saw him. He notices me standing by the door and smiles, but it doesn't reach his eyes like it usually does.

"Doc, how are ya?" he says, as he shuffles into a sitting position

"I'm good. You?" I ask, as I walk into the room.

"Fit as a fiddle." And then he coughs. It's a deep belly cough and the doctor in me winces, that's not a good cough and just as I think that, he goes into a coughing fit. He's struggling for breath, his body heaving as he tries to suck in oxygen. Racing to his side, I help him attach the breathing mask and then I take a seat and stare at him. It takes almost ten minutes for his breathing to return to normal. He pulls off the mask, "Water?" he asks, and points to the cup on his bedside table.

Picking the cup up, I hold it and the straw to his lips. He drinks and lies back down. He closes his eyes and drifts off to sleep. Not wanting to leave him alone right now, I sit back in the chair and run my fingers through my hair. Dropping my head back, I too, nod off to sleep.

I'm woken up when I feel a finger poking my cheek. Opening my eyes, I see Marvin staring at me. "Doc, you snore like a freight train."

"Do not," I defensively scoff.

"Do too," he returns like a child. "I'm surprised you didn't set any alarms off, it was that loud."

"I'm not that loud, I'm just tired. I worked a twelve hour shift last night."

"Ohh, poor baby," he teases. "When I was a spring chicken, I'd work sixteen hours a day, six days a week. Never once have I snored in my seventy-two years."

"I bet if I asked around, I'd hear that you snored." I pause and then add, "Or you'd make a cute lil' mewling sound."

"Like hell, I mewl," he scoffs. "Where's that lovely lady of yours? I prefer waking up and seeing her pretty face in that chair."

"Sorry to disappoint you, but she's at work. How about we send her a message?"

"What? Like a dick pic?"

"Marvin Marshall," a nurse scolds, as she walks in. "No respectable woman ever wants to receive one of those."

"I'm with her," I say, nodding my head toward the nurse.

"Traitor. How about a nice pic of the two of us then?" Marvin turns to the nurse. "You mind taking a pic?" he sweetly asks her.

"Not at all."

Handing my phone over to her, she takes it from me. I lean toward Marvin and wrap my arm around his shoulder. We smile for the photo. Taking my phone back from the nurse, I send it to Avery before I forget.

FLYNN: *Marvin says hi **attach photo***

"All sent."

"Good, now get out of here. I want a rest without a chugga chugga disturbing me."

Laughing, I stand up. "I'll catch ya later. Bye, Marvin."

"Later, Doc."

As I'm stepping into the elevator, my phone pings with a text.

AVERY: *My two fav men **smiling emoji***
AVERY: *Thank you for checking on him.*
FLYNN: *Happy to do it.*
FLYNN: *He seems in good spirits this morning.*

I leave out the part where I'm worried too, she doesn't need that on her plate.

FLYNN: *P.S. He wanted to send you a dick pic*
shocked face emoji
AVERY: ***Wide eye emoji***
FLYNN: *He also thinks I snore like a freight train.*
AVERY: *I plead the Fifth.*
FLYNN: *I do not snore.*
AVERY: *If you say so Thomas.*
FLYNN: *I DO NOT SNORE!*
AVERY: *Gotta get to class. Chat soon. Xo*
FLYNN: *Have a good day. Xo*

With a goofy grin on my face, I head to the doctors'

lounge to grab my things. Climbing into my car, I drive home. Forgoing a shower, I strip off and collapse into bed. I think I'm asleep before my head hits the pillow. Falling into a deep sleep, I dream of Avery...and dick pics from Marvin.

After a lonely and long week, Friday finally rolls around. Tonight, Cress and I are going out for drinks, it's been weeks since we went out. Actually, the last time we did was the first night I hooked up with Flynn.

Taking my time, I run a bath and pour myself a glass of wine. Climbing into the jasmine-scented bubbles, the warm water envelops me and I sigh. Nothing beats a relaxing bath. When the water turns cold, I climb out. Wrapping a towel around me, I head into the kitchen and pour myself another glass of wine before heading to my room to get ready. Deciding on a black, knee-length halter dress, I pair it with my trusty Louboutins. Curling my hair, I slap on some lip gloss and then I'm ready to rock.

Ordering myself an Uber, I message Cress and tell her

I'm on my way to pick her up. As I'm climbing into the car, a feeling of unease washes over me. Looking around, I see two guys, whom I've never seen before, loitering around the entrance to our building. They look out of place, one of them catches me staring at him, he nudges the other guy, and they both watch me intently as the car pulls away from the curb. A shiver runs down my spine, goosebumps appear on my skin, but as quickly as they appeared, the bumps and feeling vanish the farther we drive away from the apartment. Looking out the back window, I see them still standing there, watching as we turn the corner. Shaking my head, I sit back in my seat and start thinking about this evening, I cannot wait to let loose tonight with Cress.

Forty minutes later, after stopping to get Cress, we arrive at the Tavern. Walking inside, we make a beeline for the bar and excitement bubbles when I see the cocktail of the day is a mojito. Ordering two, I wait for our drinks and Cress goes to snag a table that was recently vacated by a couple. I lean against the bar and look toward the alcove where Flynn accosted me that first night. My body thrums as I remember what his magic fingers did to me...and what they do to me now on a regular basis. Grinning to myself, I grab our drinks and head over to Cress.

"Cheers," we both say in unison. We clink our glasses together and drink our cocktails. The tart, tangy liquid quenches my thirst and I take another sip. My phone rings, digging it out, I see Flynn's face smiling at me. "It's Flynn, give me a sec."

Cress nods and finishes her drink. She then mimics the drinking motion and makes her way to the bar to order more drinks.

"Hi, Dr. Kelly," I say, as I answer my phone.

"Good evening, Ms. Evans," he croons down the line. "How are you this fine evening?"

"I'm good. And you?"

"Glad to be finished for the week and looking forward to a weekend off. Today was dead quiet so it dragged and dragged. But I did see your number one fan."

"Marvin," I say with a smile, "How is he?"

"He's doing better. He escaped…again."

"Sounds like him. That definitely means he's doing better. I was so worried earlier this week. If you see him again, telling him I'll pop by after work one day next week."

"You really are a gem, Avery. It sounds loud, where are you?"

"Cress and I are at the Fat Fox."

"You mind if Preston and I join you ladies?"

"Not at all. I haven't seen you since last weekend and that was forever ago."

"Aww, did you miss me, baby?" He throws my taunt from earlier this week back at me.

"I'll never tell," I playfully reply.

He laughs and the timbre of the sound reverberates through my body, leaving me a wanton mess. "Sooo, just how badly did you miss me?"

"You'll see, and feel, just how badly I've missed you when you get here."

"You can't say shit like that to me when I'm not in the same room as you."

"Well, hurry up and get here so you can see and feel for yourself."

He groans and I laugh. "You are an evil minx, Avery Evans. Just you wait until I get there." *Dammit, this has backfired on me*, I think to myself when he says, "See you soon, gorgeous."

"Can't wait. Drive safely," I say in reply. Placing my phone down on the tabletop, I realize I'm beaming. Cress returns with two decadent looking cocktail glasses full of mojito. "I love you," I tell her, as she places our drinks on the table and takes her seat across from me.

"You only love me for my cocktails."

"Yeah, and?" I teasingly reply. Picking up my drink, I raise up in a toast. "To a fantabulous night with my fabulous girlfriend."

"Cheers to that." We both sip and let out an "ahhhh" as the refreshing drink dances on our tastebuds.

"What's got you so chipper?" Cress asks me, as she rocks to the beat of the music.

"Flynn and Preston are stopping by. I hope that's okay?"

Her eyes widen in delight. "Is it okay that two sexy as sin doctors want to stop by? One who happens to have a sexy as hell Irish accent, and the other could be Channing Tatum's twin, let me think about that…hell to the yes it's okay." She takes another drink and again moans. "I really need to get laid. Since Mom has Lexi for the night, I can do it without needing to fuck and chuck to get home to her."

"Get Cress laid is my mission tonight."

"I'll drink to that." She lifts her drink and salutes me. "I like this sassy side of you. Who knew you getting laid would also be good for me too? Prior to Flynn, you'd never suggest something like that."

"I know, right? I'm just so happy and I want you to be happy too."

"Ahh, thanks, babe, but try not get finger fucked here

again, save that for the privacy of home, or at the least, the car."

Choking on my drink, I shake my head. "Why did I tell you that?"

"Because you know I need to fuck vicariously through you at the moment. This dry spell is killing me. My rabbit died from overuse, and at the rate I'm going my bullet is going to burn a hole in my clit."

"Evening, ladies," Preston sneakily says from behind Cress. He steps around her and I notice his eyes are lingering on hers. Her face goes beet red as it hits her that he heard what she just said. I burst out laughing. I'm still laughing when Flynn walks over to us with two beers and two more mojitos on a tray.

"Hey, babe," I say, hopping off my stool to greet him. I place a quick kiss on his cheek but he has other ideas: he dips me back and fucks my mouth with his tongue. This kiss is totally not appropriate for being in public, but the bliss I'm currently in makes me not give a shit. I give myself over to the kiss and lose myself in all that is Flynn Kelly. Everything around me fades away. It's just the two of us.

My bubble is burst and I'm snapped back to reality when Preston teases, "Get a fuckin room, you two."

Flynn places me back on two feet and I wink at Preston as I take my seat. "Preston, great to see you again."

"You too, Avery." He turns his attention over to Cress. "Cressida, it's nice to make your acquaintance again. Since we didn't get a chance to formally chat last time, I'm Preston Knight, pediatric doctor and this thing's best friend." He flicks his thumb toward Flynn, but I notice his eyes are locked on my best friend…and hers are locked on him too.

"Thing, really?" Flynn scoffs. Preston just shrugs his shoulders but continues to focus on my best friend. Hmmmm, interesting.

"Cressida Bayliss, but my friends call me Cress," she purrs in reply, yes my best friend purrs. "I'm a mom, grade school teacher, and this sex fiend's bestie." She nods her head at me and takes a sip of her drink, as if she didn't just insult me.

My eyes bug open at her description of me.

"And are we a sex fiend too?" Preston questions her.

She nonchalantly shrugs her shoulder and takes another sip of her drink, seductively wrapping her lips around the straw. After taking a drink, she murmurs, "You already know the answer to that…" then she adds "…and you may find out again later."

Flynn laughs. Preston's face lights up and I shake my head at Crass Cress, clearly she has been keeping secrets from me. The four of us start chatting, and I notice that Preston and Cress are ignoring Flynn and me. They only have eyes for one another. My eyes are locked on the two of them when Flynn sits next to me and affectionally squeezes my knee.

Turning my attention to him I smile. "That was quite the welcome kiss."

"Only the best for my girl."

"Your girl. I like hearing you say that."

"I like saying that."

We stare at one another. Our focus is solely on each other. It isn't until I hear Preston say, "They're eye fucking each other again."

Cress replies with, "At least he isn't finger fucking her again."

My mouth drops open in shock. "Cress," I scoff, "I'm

not telling you anything anymore, and you'll have to suffice with your bullet from now on."

Preston leans into her and not so quietly whispers, "I'm more than happy to assist."

My eyes once again bug open in shock. Cress stares at him, smiles, and winks.

Flynn says, "Umm, I think I missed something."

"I wish I missed something," I say.

Cress shrugs.

Preston continues to stare at my best friend. If he was in a Bugs Bunny cartoon, hearts would be coming out of his eyes and baby Cupids would be shooting arrows into the sky.

Flynn looks lost.

And me, I just laugh. I seriously cannot remember the last time I had this much fun, and we've only been here for thirty minutes.

"Ohh, tonight is going to be a hoot."

And a hoot it was. We went from the Tavern to some new club, Tingle, which recently opened. The four of us do shots at the bar before grabbing our drinks and walking around. We find a table and settle in. My eyes gravitate to a throuple grinding together on the dance floor. She has vibrant copper hair and the two guys she's with are hot—not as hot as Flynn—but I can appreciate the opposite sex. I'm getting turned on watching them but when the music changes, they head toward the bar and out of sight.

The four of us are all well on our way to being drunk as skunks when "Acceptable in the 80's" by Calvin Harris begins playing. Flynn and Preston surprise Cress and me when they jump up and make their way to the edge of the dance floor. My mouth drops open as they both start to dance and holy-freakin-moves-Batman, the two of them are carving up the dance floor. Think Channing Tatum in *Step Up* moves—yes, I'm aware that Preston looks like him too but he also moves like him—I fucking love it.

My eyes however are locked on Flynn. His body twists and moves in sync to the beat. He's completely lost to the music, it's so good to see him relaxed. This week at the hospital has been tough for him, it's nice to see him let his hair down and chillax. This week has been tough for me too. Things with Bay have taken a turn. I'm not a fan of the new people she's hanging out with, and they keep thinking I'm her. They make me feel uncomfortable and when I confront Bay, she just laughs it off and ignores my concerns. I was ever so glad to be coming out tonight, and seeing Preston and Flynn dancing right now is making tonight amazeballs.

"Holy shit, Ave, you didn't tell me your sexy as sin doctor could dance too," Cress says.

"I had no clue. But have you seen, Preston? He's totally carving up the dance floor."

Cress and I watch as my sexy as hell boyfriend and his best friend groove away in front of us. Their moves draw in a crowd, everyone mesmerized by the two of them. The songs changes to one I don't know and both guys walk back over to us.

"Holy shit, dudes, where did you guys learn to dance like that?" Cress asks as she hands them each a beer.

"Med school," they reply in unison.

"Preston and I were the dance kings in our frat house."

"You guys were in a frat?" Cress and I ask at the same time.

"Jinx," she says, I shrug and turn my attention to Flynn.

He nods. "Yeah, Preston and I were Phi Kappa Psi at Stanford."

"I did not pick you as a frat guy."

He shrugs his shoulders. "There's still a lot you don't know about me, Avery Evans."

"So tell me then, what else don't I know about you, Flynn Kelly?"

"Weeeell, I'm crazy about this sexy as sin school teacher, and I'm pretty sure she's crazy about me too."

Shrugging my shoulders nonchalantly, I grin at him. "Go on."

"I love that when I touch her here…" He steps to me and drags his fingertip up my thigh. "…she quivers with desire and her panties dampen."

"What else?" I huskily breathe and my panties do indeed dampen as he continues to draw circles on my thigh.

He leans into my ear. "I cannot wait to get you back to my place where I'm going to strip you naked, even though this little black dress is fucking divine on you. I need you naked so I can fuck you repeatedly. All.Night.Long. Just like our first night together."

Swallowing deeply, I look into his eyes. "I'm down with that." Reaching up, I hook my arm around his neck and bring his lips to mine and kiss him deeply. The sound of Preston slamming his beer down on the table pulls us apart. Looking over, I see him ask Cress to dance and she blushes. Yes, my best friend blushes, but she takes his outstretched hand and they head toward the dance floor. Watching them, my eyes are focused on the chemistry radiating between them.

"Wow, those two are, ummm…" Flynn says, his eyes

looking at our two friends dirty—almost dry humping—dance with each other to "Pony" by Genuwine.

"Yep," I say, nodding my head. "Wanna show them how it's done?" I sexily purr.

"Hell yes. Any chance to have my hands all over your sexy body sounds perfect to me. Let's go get our groove on."

Laughing at his reply, I place my drink on the high-top table. "Don't ever say that again."

"Don't fret, don't plan on saying it again. As soon as the words left my mouth I instantly regretted them." We both laugh.

Leaning into him, I whisper with a wink, "I'll spank you later."

Gabbing his hand, I pull him onto the dance floor just as "Sexy Back" by JT starts to play. We begin to bump and grind and we take on Cress and Preston in a dance-off. Somehow it becomes Cress and me against them. Flynn and Preston totally win, they left Cress and me for dead, but watching Flynn dance is totally fucking hot.

The rest of the night flies by and it's the most fun I've had in a long time. We dance. We slam back shots like we are in college. We dance some more. We eat gross greasy food that can only to be consumed when you're drunk and then we drink some more.

At stupid o'clock in the morning, Flynn and I leave Cress and Preston at the club, they are still dancing and the two of them are getting hotter and hotter the more we drink. We stumble back to Flynn's place and once inside, we ravish each other's bodies multiple times before we pass out from exhaustion just as the sun is rising.

When I wake several hours later, I'm wrapped in Flynn's embrace. My body aches from head to toe, and I'm not sure if it's from all the dancing last night or the multiple orgasms I had once we got back here. My head is pounding and my stomach is queasy, damn shots.

Sliding out of bed, I slip on his shirt from last night and head to the kitchen to make some coffee and get some water, my mouth feels like a dirty ashtray. The only downside to a big night out is the morning after. I've just turned the coffee machine on when my phone rings. Looking down I see that it's Bay.

"Hey, Bay."

"Where are you?" she snarls.

"Good morning to you too."

"Whatevs, where are you?"

"Not home." I don't tell her where I am because I don't want any grief from her concerning Flynn.

"Well, I need a ride. I drank too much last night and I need you to come and get me."

"No, Bay, I'm sorry, I can't."

Flynn comes up behind me and wraps his arms around me. Cupping my boobs, he squeezes them and a moan breaks free.

"Ugh, seriously, Ave? You can't wait until I'm off the phone?"

Even though I'm holding my phone to my ear, I totally forgot she was there. "Sorry, I'm busy, Bay. You'll have to Uber it."

"Some sister you are. I'd be there for you if you called me in need."

"Yeah, right," I scoff. "Grab an Uber and I'll see you when I get home." Another moan slips out when Flynn pinches my nipple.

"Is that sexy as sin doctor with you?"

"No," I snap, but it's not convincing at all.

"He'll be mine soon," she softly says, and before I can tell her off, she hangs up on me.

"Gah!" I shout, as I throw my phone on the counter. "I hate her stinkin' guts." I pause, and then playfully tack on, "You make me vomit. You're scum between my toes. Love Alfalfa." I laugh as I recite this verse and when I spin around to look at Flynn, he's looking at me like I have two heads. "It's from *Little Rascals*." He's still looking at me with a blank stare on his face, and I realize he has never seen the movie. "You've never seen it, have you?"

"Seen what?" he asks, shrugging his shoulders, utterly confused right now.

"*Little Rascals*, the movie."

He shakes his head side to side. "Nope. Never seen or heard of it."

I scoff in fake shock, "Well, then we need to rectify this. Later today, me. You. *Little Rascals*. A bottle of red and popcorn."

"Can we be naked?"

I laugh at his request. "Sure, why not."

"Perfect," he reiterates, "later we will watch *Little Rascals*, naked, while drinking red wine and eating popcorn. But first, coffee."

"I like that plan."

We sit at the island, drinking our coffee, and we chat about the movie. I pretty much tell him everything that happens since I know the movie from start to finish. Baylor and I loved the movie growing up, we must have watched it a million times over the years.

Finishing our coffee, we head back to bed and sleep for a few more hours. Seriously, I am never drinking again. I'm too old to party 'til the wee hours and then fuck 'til the sun comes up. Not that I've ever done that before, but I can unequivocally say, I'll do it again because last night was amazing and anyone who says they are never drinking again is a big fat liar, because they totally will drink excessively again.

After our nap, we order Chinese and eat our weight in Mongolian beef and watch *Little Rascals*. Like I agreed, we watch it naked while drinking red wine—see, I drank again—and eating popcorn. I recite just about every line and then we make sweet, sweet love on the sofa. I completely forget about all my concerns with my sister because I'm with Flynn.

He hops up to refill our wine and as I watch his naked ass, I realize that no longer am I falling for Dr. Kelly, I've fallen head over heels, ass over tits, in love with this sexy as sin Irish doctor, and I've never been happier.

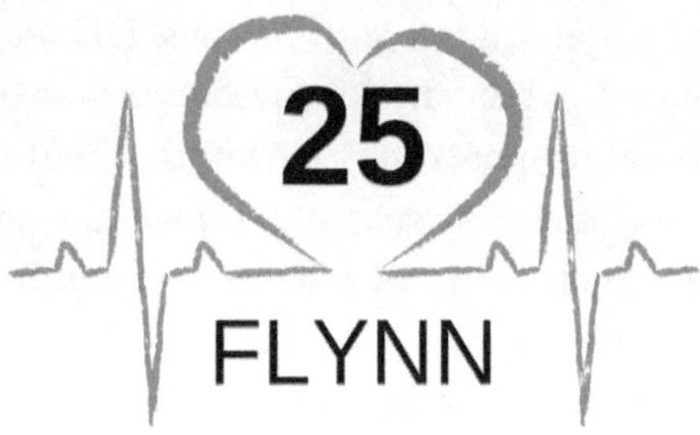

25

FLYNN

Grabbing a glass of water, I sigh when I realize it's been three days since I saw Avery in person. Seems three days is my limit before I turn into a total girl and start whining like a little bitch. We had a quick FaceTime chat earlier but that's not the same. She left my place Sunday at dinnertime after we spent the most of the weekend together. Apart from a few text messages and our Face-Time, I've missed seeing her…damn double shifts and life getting in the way.

Even though I'm dog-tired, I want to see her. Picking up my phone, I go to call and see if she's free for dinner, but I'm interrupted by a knock at the door. Walking over, I open the door and I'm pleasantly surprised to see Avery standing there. My mouth drops open at the sight before me. She's wearing a figure-hugging, pink dress that leaves NOTHING to the imagination, I've never seen her dress like this before. "Fuck me, you are gorgeous."

"I know," she replies.

Shaking my head at her cheeky response, my eyes once again rake over her body—shoot me—I'm male and my sexy as hell woman is here, and suddenly, I'm not so tired anymore. I've never seen her like this before. There's something different with her tonight but fuck me, I'll take it. She steps around me and walks, no, saunters in and takes a seat at the breakfast bar. She crosses her legs, ala Sharon Stone in *Basic Instinct* and I'm pretty sure she isn't wearing any panties. I'm totally digging this sexy vixen version of Avery.

"What are you doing here?" I ask, as I walk over to the wine fridge and grab a bottle of white. *It's after five and we can order* in I tell myself, as I uncork the bottle. Grabbing two glasses from the cupboard, I pour us each a glass and hand one to her. Her fingers brush mine and the zing I usually feel isn't there tonight, maybe it's because I've just finished a twenty-four hour shift and I'm shattered.

"I missed you," she says, "It's been too long since I've seen you."

"You FaceTimed me at lunch today."

Her eyes bug open and then she sexily whines, "That was forever ago."

"You are too cute."

"I know," she replies again. Something is definitely off with her tone tonight. I put it down to being super tired, I'm not even enjoying my wine and this is my favorite.

"Look, Ave lass, I'm sorry to do this, but I'm shattered

after my shift. Can we do this tomorrow? After I've gotten some sleep."

She looks at me, and her face it etched with rejection. I hate that I put that look on her face, but I know if I ask her to stay, I won't be getting to sleep for a few more hours, and I just can't, as much as it pains me. I need sleep.

"Fine," she snaps, "but can you drop me home first? I got an Uber here."

"Of course," I say, confused as to why she'd Uber it here, she doesn't usually Uber it unless she's drinking. "Are you okay?" I question.

"I'm fine," she snaps again, clearly she's tired too.

We head down to the parking garage and when she climbs in, I once again get a view of her pantyless ass. I'm close to taking her back upstairs but something is stopping me from doing so.

The car ride back to her place is quiet. It's kind of awkward, but I put it down to me being a complete zombie right now, actually, I'm surprised I didn't crash on the way over here. Pulling up outside her apartment building, I walk around the hood. After helping her out, she links her arm with mine and we walk inside. We climb into the elevator and ride up to her floor. Again it's silent and awkward. The doors open and we step out. She's digging in her purse for her keys, banging on the door as she does so. Suddenly, as if she's heard something, her head snaps up and she looks at me. Her eyes take on a glint I've never seen before. She steps toward me, drapes her arms over my shoulders and gazes into my eyes. She starts leaning in when the apartment door swings opens. A smirk appears on her face and we both turn our heads. The person standing in the doorway looks shocked. Her gaze darting back and forth between us, and then her eyes well with tears, and a sinking feeling develops in my guts.

"Flynn. Bay." She steps into the hall with us. "What's going on?"

What.

The.

Fuck.

"Avery?" I question, looking between the two of them.

"Hey, Sis," Baylor says from in front of me.

Immediately, I step back and push Baylor away from me. My eyes dart between them and suddenly, everything makes sense now. The awkwardness. The unease. No spark, it's because I was with Baylor and not Avery. Had I not been dog-tired, I would have known immediately.

Turning to Avery, my hearts breaks when I see the devastation on her face. "Avery," I plead, "I'm—"

She raises her hand. "No. Don't." On a sob, she blubbers, "Just go, Flynn."

She turns on her heel and walks into the apartment. My eyes follow her as she somberly races into her bedroom. My heart shattering with each step she takes away from me.

"Well, that was perfect," Baylor smugly says from beside me. "Call me," she sweetly says as she steps toward me. She rests her palms on my chest and places a kiss on my cheek. Turning on her heel, she walks toward the elevators and steps into the car we just exited.

Shaking my head, I watch as the doors close and then I hear it, a gut-wrenching sound emits from inside the apartment. Racing in, I slam the door behind me and make my way to Avery's room, her sobs getting louder and louder.

Standing at the doorway, my heart breaks at the scene before me. Avery is lying on her bed in the fetal position, tears cascading down her cheeks. She's completely shattered and it's all because of me, and her sister. I can't take it. I step into her bedroom and plead, "Ave lass, please."

"Don't, Ave lass, me!" I scream, my heart is shattering in half right now. Wiping at my eyes, I refuse to cry. He doesn't deserve my tears, I sit up and cross my legs. Taking a deep breath, I lift my gaze and glare at him. "You were..." I can't finish my sentence, the tears start again and they pour like an avalanche down my cheeks. "You were about to kiss my sister," I sniffle. Voicing that out loud shatters my heart into a million tiny fragments. "How could you?"

"I thought she was you!" he shouts in defense. Does he really think so little of me that he would try that lame excuse?

"Please," I scoff. "Don't insult me, Flynn. If you want

her, go for it. I know she's vivacious and out there, and I'm—"

"Perfect," he says, as he strides over to me, eating up the distance in a few steps. Dropping to his knees in front of me, he takes my hands in his and grips them tightly, squeezing in an oddly reassuring way. "Avery Evans, you are perfect, absolutely-fucking-perfect and...and...I love you. I fucking love you."

My mouth drops open at his declaration. I've gone from hurt and anger to shock and awe.

"Avery, I love you." He climbs up onto the bed, shuffling to his knees and with my hands still in his; he stares intently into my eyes. "From the moment I laid eyes on you, I was smitten. I had to have you. I had you and then you left, but then fate bought us back together and I was once again bewildered by you. You are the air in my lungs. The beat of my heart. You are my everything, Avery Evans." He pauses. "Ave lass, I love you."

Blinking rapidly, I process the words he just said to me. Words that resonate deep in my soul, I believe and I feel every one of those words. "I love you too, Flynn Kelly."

Wrapping my arms around his neck, I slam my lips against his and pull him toward me. Our bodies collide. We become one. This kiss is electric, it's different from the many before. The love between us radiates around my room. It envelops us and swallows us whole. Nothing else matters except for Flynn and me and our love for one for another.

Falling to the mattress with our lips fused, we let our

love flow between us. I'm blissfully in love with this man and he loves me back. I love him with every fiber in my being. Nothing and no one can tear us apart.

After our declaration of love, Flynn and I lie on my bed in each other's arms. The sound of the front door opening, startles us. Baylor giggles when some guy says something and thankfully, they head to her bedroom, slamming her bedroom door with enough force to shake my room. Letting out a sigh, I look to Flynn. He knows from the look on my face that I need to get out of the apartment. Without saying a word, he lifts me out of bed. My legs wrap around him and I hang on like a monkey. He exits my apartment and carries me down to his car and away from Baylor.

The beating of his heart calms me, I'm reluctant to let him go. I want to stay in his arms forever, and as if he can read my mind, he says. "As much as I love having you in my arms, I need to let you go so I can drive us back to my place."

Nodding my head, I unwrap my legs from his waist and lower my feet to the ground. He opens the car door for me and before I hop in, I look to him. "I love you, Flynn."

"And I love you, Avery. Now get in."

Climbing in, I strap myself in and we head to Flynn's and away from my deceitful sister. My thoughts are a jumbled mess but they keep coming back to those three words, I love you. Who knew three little words, eight letters could hold so much power?

Arriving at his place, Flynn parks in his spot and we lace our fingers together and head up to his apartment. We don't say anything, the silence is peaceful. We step into his penthouse and a calmness washes over me, that is until I see the open bottle of wine and two glasses sitting on the island counter. I stop midstep and my eyes snap to his, my blood simmering and hurt courses through my veins; she was here. Any calmness I had evaporates and rage takes its place.

"Nothing happened!" he yells. "She turned up here just as I got home from the hospital. My mind isn't functioning properly. I've been awake for over twenty-six hours now. I honestly thought she was you. You two are strikingly similar but also different, and I sensed something was off but I just put it down to being overtired." He pauses. "I'm so sorry, Ave." Turning to face me, he goes to take my hand in his, but I step back. He looks to me and pleads, "I promise you, Avery, nothing happened between us. Please believe me!"

As I stare at him, I see the remorse and guilt he feels in his eyes. Stepping over to him, I cup his cheek in my palm. "I believe you." Relief floods his face at my words. "Flynn, you are mine," I emphasize the word mine, "even when you're dead tired and your mind is playing tricks on you. Your heart sensed something was up because it beats for me and only me. Just like mine beats only for you." Wrapping my arms around his shoulders, I rest my head on his chest. "You are mine, Flynn Kelly, forever and eternity," I whisper, as I close my eyes and snuggle into him.

He wraps his around me in return and kisses my head. He whispers, "I'm yours, Avery, forever and eternity." We silently hug one another. It's nice. It's perfect, and it's exactly what we need right now. I know without a doubt that he's telling the truth, but I'm so confused as to why Baylor would do this to me. To him. Something is amiss with her but that's something for another day. Lifting my head, I look up at him. "Flynn, take me to bed," I huskily whisper as I nuzzle his chin.

"With pleasure," he growls, tightening his embrace around me.

Scooping his arms under my legs, he lifts me up and carries me bridal style into his bedroom. He places me on my feet at the end of the bed. He lowers his lips to mine and gently kisses me. Pulling back, I whisper, "Be right back."

Walking over to the en suite bathroom, I close the door behind me and stare at my reflection and grin. *Flynn loves me and I love him.* Cue freak-out, but no freak-out occurs because this is meant to be. I'm happy and content with this declaration. Taking a deep breath, I pull my shirt over my head and slide my jeans down my legs; ever so thankful I wore a sexy matching set today.

Opening the door, I sexily step through and when I look to the bed, I smile. Flynn is sound asleep, snoring loudly, like he does when he's super exhausted. Walking over to the bed, I drop to my knees and remove his shoes and socks. Then I manage to get his jeans down and I begin to unbutton his shirt. He stirs. "Ave lass, I'm sorry," he sleepily says.

"Shhhh," I whisper. "Go back to sleep, baby."

He sits up and his eyes pop open when he sees what I'm wearing. "Ave, you are so fucking gorgeous," he hungrily says, his eyes immediately drooping closed before his head falls to my stomach, once again asleep.

"Sleep, baby," I say, running my fingers through his hair. Kissing his head, I whisper, "I'll be here in the morning."

Sliding his shirt down his arms, I gently push him backward and he drops back to the mattress, managing to pull me down with him. He rolls to his side and I snuggle into him, spooning. He's out cold, snoring like a freight train. Me? I'm wide awake and my mind is firing on all cylinders. Why did Bay do this? What is wrong with her? And what I can do to get my sister back?

Eventually my eyes become heavy and my last thought before I drift off to sleep is that the man I'm currently snuggling with loves me, just as much as I love him. Bay and her pettiness be damned.

Waking up with Avery in my bed is fast becoming my favorite way to start my day. Rolling to my side, my eyes roam over her body. Her sexy as sin body is currently encased in a black satin bra and panties combo. The sun is just rising and in the morning light, Avery looks radiant. Tracing my finger down her breastbone, ever so gently, her skin prickles under my touch and her hazel eyes flutter open, the green vibrant in the early morning light.

"Morning, beautiful."

"Morning," she huskily says, smiling at me. Even sleepy, she's gorgeous.

Leaning toward her, I place my lips against hers. Rolling her to her back, I roll on top of her, cocooning her body with mine and deepening our kiss. Sliding my hand down her side, the moment is interrupted by Avery's phone's alarm.

"I have to get to work," she sadly says. "Rain check?"

"Abso-fuckin-lutely, BUT you need to wear this again," I say, skimming my finger over the satin circling her nipple.

She closes her eyes and moans before huskily whispering, "Deal."

Lowering my head, I kiss the tip of her nose and we climb out of bed and get dressed. I drop Avery home and after a longer than necessary goodbye kiss, she climbs out of my car. I sit and watch the woman I love walk into her building. The door closes behind her and I realize how close I came to losing her yesterday…and all because of her sister. Shaking my head, I decide to head to the hospital to spend some time with Marvin before my shift starts, I'd rather be around him than on my own at the moment.

After a crazy few days, it's finally Saturday. Thankfully there have been no more doppelgänger incidents. Ave and I have FaceTimed each morning before she heads off to work, but it's not the same as a face-to-face visit; man, life getting in the way of my woman and me is a drag. I may have gone overboard with gifts this week, wanting to reaffirm to Avery that I love her and only her. To her school, I sent a huge bunch of tulips. To her home, a delivery from Agent Provocateur, that's more of a gift for me but potato/vodka. There was also a voucher sent from Allyu Spa for couple's spa day package—just need to find the time for both of us to be free—and finally, an invite to spend the night with me tonight.

Just before lunch, Ave arrives with pizza and beer; man, I love this woman. After devouring the pizza, we decide on a lazy day at home before our dinner date tonight, where I surprise Avery with new a dress and more lingerie from Agent Provocateur. I take her back to Rococo's and just like our first night here, we have an amazing time. Followed by an equally amazing sexy night in bed when we get home.

The next morning, Avery is up before me and I'm pleasantly awakened by the smell of breakfast. She cooks us pancakes and we eat naked on the couch, watching another of Avery's all time fav movies, *Empire Records*.

It's the perfect Sunday morning until Avery receives a call from Baylor. She stares at her phone for a few moments before she takes a deep breath and answers, putting it on speaker.

"Hey, Bay."

"Avery." Her tone is curt and rude.

Then it's silent, I can feel the tension building in Avery from where I'm sitting next to her. I take her hand in mine and gently squeeze, giving her the courage to go on. She takes a deep breath. "What do you want, Bay?"

"Wondering where you are? Are you with Cress commiserating over the demise your relationship with Flynn?" she says, her voice laced with such venom.

"No, I'm not." Avery defiantly replies, her voice strong. "Actually, I'm at Flynn's right now. I've spent the weekend with him."

"Even though he cheated on you?"

"He didn't cheat. He told me nothing happened between you two."

"Of course he'd say that, he's—"

"Bay, stop with the fucking lies. I've had it. Just stop."

"Enjoy it while you can, Ave. You won't get your happily ever after…mark my words."

The line goes dead. Looking over to Avery, I see that she's gutted. Wanting to distract her, I tell her to go get changed. She slips into her jeans that I love and a dark pink off-the-shoulder sweater thing.

We head to my car. "Can you tell me where we're going?" she begs, as we pull out of the underground parking garage.

"Don't you want a surprise?"

"Kinda. Sorta. Not really." She pauses. "Pleease tell me. I'll make it worth your while?" She suggestively raises her eyebrows at me.

"Lass, you'll be getting sex when we get back, so that's not really a bargaining tool at all."

"Fine," she huffs; crossing her arms across her chest she pouts like a child. It's cute but seeing her down cuts me deep.

"I hate seeing you sad like this so I'll tell you," I concede, and she instantly smiles. "We're heading to the hospital to see Marvin. I thought a visit with him would cheer you up since he always manages to make you smile."

"Ohh, Flynn, thank you," she cheerfully says.

As soon as we step into his room, both of them light up and seeing the joy on her face warms my Irish heart.

We stopped at his favorite bakery on the way and grabbed a dozen glazed donuts before stopping at Starbucks across the road from the hospital for coffees. The nurse isn't too happy to see Marvin shoveling a donut— it's actually his fourth but from the scowl on her face, I won't be bringing that up. "Marvin Marshall, you know that donuts aren't allowed on your diet." The nurse looks to me and now I'm scared. "And you, Dr. Kelly," she points a finger at me, "should know better."

Avery giggles from where she's sitting and it's nice to see her relaxed, so I take the verbal lashing with a grain of salt. If my girl is happy, it's the least that I can do. Marvin manages to win the nurse over by offering her a donut. "You were a total heartbreaker back in the day, weren't you, Marvin?" I ask, as the nurse walks out of his room, nibbling on her sweet treat.

"You betcha I was."

He looks to Avery. "If I was forty years younger, you and I would have a ball together."

"I'm sure we would," she playfully replies.

Marvin looks to me. "You look after this one, she's special. What she sees in a snoring freight train like you is beyond me."

We all laugh, at my expense. And the barbs continue throughout the afternoon. We spend the next few hours playing cards with Marvin and listening to his wild stories. He's lead an amazing life. We say our goodbyes and when we climb into my car, Avery looks to me, and hesitantly asks, "Can you, ummm, drop me home?"

"Ohh," I say, deflated that she isn't staying at my place again.

"I just want to grab a few things so I don't have to rush in the morning."

Relief washes over me. "Sure can, babycakes."

"Babycakes, really?"

"Too much?"

"Just a little."

We've just pulled up to her place when my phone rings

and it's the hospital. They are short staffed in the ER and need me to cover a shift. Reluctantly, I say goodbye to Avery, after getting her to agree to get her things and head to my place to wait for me. She climbs out of my car and I watch until she's safely inside. Then I head back to where we just came from, but our plan doesn't work out quite like we expected and nothing will be the same again.

FLYNN HAS JUST LEFT AND I'M FEELING PRETTY GREAT RIGHT now, actually I'm more than great. I'm on cloud a billion at this specific moment in time. The afternoon with Marvin was just what I needed, AND I've decided the Bay issue is a non-issue. I'm not going to let her ruin this for me. I've never been this happy before and nothing, I mean nothing, is going to stand in the way of my happiness, and if I know Bay, that will piss her off more than rolling over in defeat. It breaks my heart that my own sister, my twin, is trying to tear us apart but if anything, her interference has brought Flynn and I closer together. So in a way, it's a blessing in disguise.

What I'm struggling with is that she won't talk to me. Something is up. Normally, we tell each other everything but at the moment, she's a different person and I don't like this version of my sister. Yes, we've always been different, but we've always had each other's back and we'd never do anything to purposely hurt one another. I just wish she'd talk to me, I want my twinsie back.

Pouring myself a glass of wine, I think about Flynn and find myself grinning, like I do most times I think about him. We may be opposites in many ways, but I think that's what makes us, well, us. We balance each other out, like yin and yang. He brings me out of my shell and I like the version of me that has surfaced. Without him, I'd still be shy and timid, but since meeting him, I'm a lot more outgoing and I'm happy, happier than I've ever been. I'm not going to let Flynn get away, if I have my way, no one is going to stop me from keeping my man. I've said it before and I'll say it again, I'm swooning hard for Dr. Kelly and for the first time ever, I'm not going down without a fight. I will fight tooth and nail for what's mine, and Flynn is mine. I love him with all my heart and I'll do anything for the man I love.

I just hope our love for one another is strong enough to weather any storm which comes our way. "Bring it on," I say to the empty room, and I feel good saying this, even if it is only to myself.

Just as I've made this declaration, the person behind my recent anxiety and discomfort walks in, well, she saunters in as if her shit doesn't stink. I haven't seen her since we had our major blowout showdown. We've been ships passing in the night and I'm happy to have it like that. Never before have I not wanted to see Bay. Sure, we've had our differences but at the end of the day, we are sisters and love each other. We've always been able to overcome our hurdles, but I'm not sure if it's possible this time. She's never maliciously hurt me before, and I don't think I can easily forgive and forget this time.

My eyes track her movements, she seems tense and stressed. The twin instinct in me rears to life and wants to help her but I know Bay, if I push, she'll clam up and become spiteful, well, more spiteful that she has been lately. I need her to come to me on her own terms, and that means taking the brunt of her outbursts and putting on a brave smiling face. She finally notices me. "Well, well, well, look who's sulking at home, drinking wine like the loser she is." She sashays into the kitchen, dropping her Prada—fake—handbag onto the granite countertop.

"Bay," I say, lifting my wine to my lips so I don't say something I'll regret.

She stares at me, her lip lifts in a facetious way and I just know what's about to spill from her lips is going to piss me off, possibly hurt me more. "I had THE best night and morning—" she pauses and glares at me, "but I won't bore you with the sexy gritty details."

My blood begins to boil at what she's insinuating, if it had been last week, I would have fallen for her lies and deceit regarding her and Flynn, but not this week. This week I have all the information and she can no longer hurt me with her deception. I knew she could be cruel, she's always had a bit of a nasty streak but never with me. I never thought I'd be on the receiving end of her nastiness. She's always had my back. We were twinsies forever but now, she's going out of her way to hurt me.

"Sounds nice." Not giving her anything, I place my glass on the counter and half-heartedly smile at her as I step toward her. "I'm heading to my room." I dart around her but I don't get far, she grips my arm, digging her fingers in.

"You won't keep him, Ave," she snarls. Lifting my gaze to her, I see nothing reflecting back in her eyes. The final knife in my armor is when she adds, "I'll see to it."

Taking a deep breath, I ignore her and race to my bedroom. Slamming the door behind me, I slide down the wood and breathe deeply. My eyes well with tears but I hold them back, she doesn't deserve my tears. Lowering my head to my knees, I sigh deeply and take big, deep calming breaths. "Why do you hate me so much, Bay?" I whisper, wiping away a lone tear that's managed to break free. I stare into my room at nothing in particular and my phone beeps with a text. Lifting myself up, I dig it out of my pocket and smile when I see who it's from.

FLYNN: *Miss you already, sexy lady.*
AVERY: *I needed that.*
AVERY: *You know who just came home.*
FLYNN: *Do you need me to come back over?*

My face breaks out in a smile at his offer. I'd love nothing more than for him to come back, but he's at work and I don't want him and Bay under the same roof. I don't trust her one bit when it comes to Flynn.

AVERY: *Thanks, but no thanks. I'm going to crawl into bed and watch Netflix. Besides, you need to play doctor and save some lives.*
FLYNN: *We can snuggle together and watch Netflix.*
FLYNN: *I've heard I'm a good snuggler. #JustSayin*

I laugh at his reply.

AVERY: *I know you are.*

AVERY: *But I'll be fine. Other people need you more than I do right now.*
FLYNN: *Reluctantly I say fine, BUT I'm taking you out for dinner tomorrow after I sleep.*
AVERY: *Sounds wonderful. Can't wait! **blowing kiss emoji***
FLYNN: *Sleep well, beautiful. Love you. Xo*

Staring at my phone, I focus on the 'Xo' part of his text and once again I find myself grinning. Never before have those two letters, or those three beautiful words meant so much to me.

AVERY: *Nite nite. Love you too. Xo*

Standing up, I change into my pajamas and hop into bed. Closing my eyes, I drift off to sleep with a goofy grin on my face. Happy. Content and in love.

Waking the next morning, I feel refreshed and relaxed. Picking up my phone, I see I have a text from Cress.

CRESS: *Wanna do something crazy today?*

Shaking my head, I dial and she picks up on the second ring. She doesn't give me a chance to talk, she dives right into her crazy plan. Staring at the ceiling, I listen to her. Pondering her words, I sit up in bed. "I can't believe I'm saying this but sure, I'm in." She squeals in my ear and we agree to meet up in an hour's time.

Hanging up, I grab a quick shower and slip into a pair of light wash denim jeans, a black racer back tank, and my navy Chucks. Filling my to-go coffee mug, I race out to meet Cress for our crazy adventure.

Two hours later, I'm sitting across from Cress in a restaurant, after our adventure we decided to get brunch. After demolishing the most amazing three egg omelette, I sit back and stare at Cress. "I cannot believe I let you talk me into it."

"I cannot believe you agreed." We both laugh. "But seriously, Avery, I have never seen you so happy. I think a certain sexy Irish doctor was just the medicine you needed."

"And I think a certain Channing Tatum looking doctor is the prescription you need. One of these days, you are going to have to tell me what's up between you two."

She mimes zipping her lips. "My lips are sealed." She pauses and then leans forward. "But I will say—" She doesn't get to finish, because some crazy chick comes up to our table and slaps me hard across the face. "You bitch," she snarls. "It's all your fault. I wish Kye had never met you."

Before I have a chance to reply, she's storming away.

"What the fuck was that?" Cress asks, her eyes flicking between the retreating form of psycho Barbie and me. "And who the fuck is Kye?"

Shaking my head, I cup my stinging cheek. "Beats me who Kye is. " The name Kye is familiar but I cannot place it or him. "But, man, does she have a wicked left hook."

Cress looks back at me and shakes her head. We finish our brunch and then say our goodbyes. I stroll back to my car and think about the events of today. The crazy events of today, I still can't believe Cress convinced me to do it, but this is the new carefree, fun Avery and she had an absolute blast today.

Driving home with a smile on my face, I think how crazy my life is right at this moment. Meeting Flynn.

Falling in love. The discontent with Baylor. Crazy Cress and our adventures together. Hanging with Marvin. My life is mostly perfect right now.

Parking my car, I decide to take the stairs as I'm excessively full from brunch. My phone pings with a text before I enter the stairwell. Digging it out of my bag, I smile when I see it's from Flynn.

FLYNN: *I need to see you.*
FLYNN: *Feel free to wear that black satin number.*
FLYNN: *Please come over. **begging emoji***
FLYNN: ***begging emoji***
FLYNN: ***sad emoji***
AVERY: *Be there soon. **wink wink***

Racing into the stairwell, I hall ass up the stairs, two at a time. I'm huffing and puffing by time I reach our floor. Running into the apartment, I quickly change into my black satin bra and panties set, as per Flynn's request, and then I slip on my purple dress from our first official date. Applying some lips gloss, I run my fingers through my hair. Blowing myself a kiss in the mirror, I can't believe how great I look.

Deciding to be brazen, before I exit my room, I pull my dress down and snap a sexy image of my shoulder with just a hint of my bra and a sexy pout. I quickly text it to Flynn and before I've left my room, I get a reply.

FLYNN: ***eyes emoji***
FLYNN: *Get your ass over here!*
FLYNN: *Now!*
AVERY: *Just leaving. Love you.*

Exiting my room, I grab my bag and car keys. Opening the front door, I come to a halt. I'm met with a burly bald-headed man and his skinny runt of sidekick and then it hits me, these are the guys from outside the building the other week.

"Can I help you?" I ask.

"Baylor."

"No, I'm not her. I'm—"

"Shut it, bitch. We want what's ours!" the bald guy bellows, spittle flying through the air. He stares me down and that prickly feeling from the other day appears. "NOW!" he growls, slamming his fist into the doorframe.

"I'm sorr—" But I don't get to finish that sentence, the skinny guy zaps me with a Taser.

Dropping to my knees, my body flinches and coils from the electrical shock. Glancing up at him, the elevator dings and in a panic the guy rears back his leg and kicks me in the ribs and in the face. The force snaps my head back and it hits the doorframe with a thud. The last thing I remember is faintly hearing my name being yelled before I'm zapped again. And then everything goes black.

BAYLOR

WELL FUCK, THIS ISN'T WORKING OUT HOW I PLANNED. I needed Avery to be sad and locked away in her room, or crying at Cress's house. But no, she's loved up with Flynn and because of me; my actions are going to catch up with her. Maybe I need to stop with the flirting and push her toward him, that way she will move in with him and I can be free to live my life without worrying about her.

Fuck, how did it come to this?

Last night, seeing her strong and not wilting, I was kinda proud of her. Normally she'd roll over but since meeting this Flynn guy, she's changed. But then so I have, the main difference is she's changed for the better. Me? I've changed for the worse and I've turned into someone I barely recognize anymore. If I'm honest, I don't like who

I've turned into. I need to do something, but what? I'm in too deep now.

Picking up my coffee, I look around our apartment and realize I'm lonely and unhappy, I want to be the old me again. I wonder where Avie is right now. And that thought hurts; we always used to know where the other was. Flopping onto the sofa, my mind drifts to when things were good with us...

...Avie and I have are having a baking day. We are going to bake up a storm. Avie starts getting out the ingredients and I walk over to the sound system. Switching it on, I click into Spotify and crank up the tunes. "The Piña Colada Song" comes on and we sing along as we get our Martha Stewart on. We bake chocolate chip peanut butter cookies, triple chocolate muffins, and banana bread. While the treats are cooling, we whip up a lasagne for dinner tonight and Ave makes her famous caramel dumplings.

Looking around the kitchen I smile, Avie and I haven't had a day like this in forever. We had so much fun but right now, the kitchen looks like a winter wonderland. There's white powder all through the kitchen. We may have had a flour fight while making the béchamel sauce for the lasagne, but I'm not worried about the mess because my neat freak sister—bless her little neat cotton socks—will go all Suzy Homemaker and have every speck cleaned up before I even start to wash the conditioner out of my hair.

As that memory fades, I realize I need to change my life and I need to do it now. I want more baking days with her, I want the old us back. With a sigh, I come to the conclusion I need to change now. To say I'm in over my head is the understatement of the millennium. It started out innocently, but as time went on and the thrill subsided,

I'd find new ways to get my thrills and now, well, now I'm screwed and not in the good, panting, sweaty naked way.

When Kye died, that was when I realized how deep in I was, but how the fuck am I going to get out of this? I tried to push Avery away to protect her, but that backfired spectacularly. Now she's hurt and lying unconscious in a hospital bed because of me, and what do I do? I pretend to be her to save my own ass.

This is spiraling out of control. I need to come up with a plan and I need to do it fast because when she wakes up, I'm screwed.

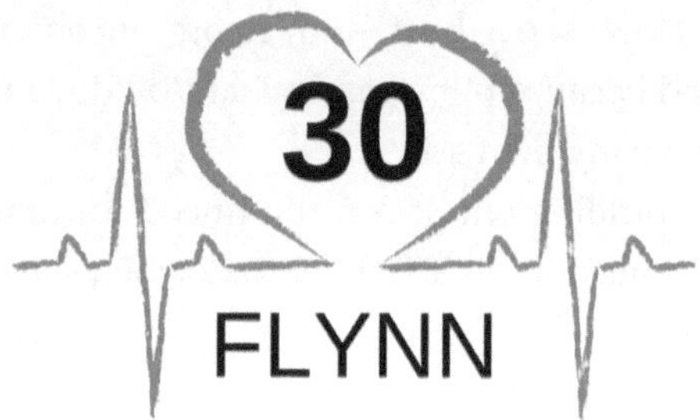

Holy fucking shit!

The image that Avery just sent me is burnt into my retinas, and ever since I opened that message, my cock has been rock-hard. I'm pacing in front of my door, eagerly awaiting her arrival.

Thirty minutes pass and she still isn't here. I put it down to traffic.

Another thirty minutes passes and now I'm antsy. I feeling of unease settles in my stomach.

Sixty minutes have passed and now I'm worried. That unease has magnified tenfold and I'm worried as all fuck. Picking up my phone, I dial Avery but it rings out and goes to voicemail. "Ave lass, it's me, please call me back as soon as you get this message. I'm worried. I love you."

Throwing my phone on the island countertop, I stare at my front door, willing it to open. With each second that passes, the feeling of dread intensifies in my gut. Just as I'm about to call her again, my phone lights up and it's her. "Ave lass—"

"Flynn…" she blubbers, "it's…it's Bay."

"What's wrong? Where are you?" I knew something wasn't right, I should have gone to her place rather than waiting here like a lovesick fool.

"I'm at Western General." She sounds so broken, I know she's on the outs with her sister right now, but at the end of the day, Baylor is her twin.

"I'm on my way."

"Hurry."

Before she'd hung up, I was already racing toward the door.

Thirty minutes later, I race into the ER and immediately my eyes land on Avery. She's accompanied by two police officers. Taking a deep calming breath, I get myself under control as I walk toward them, eating up the distance quickly. She looks up and when her gaze lands on mine, a look washes over her before she throws herself at me. "Flynn," she cries into my chest. My arms instinctively wraps around her. She falls apart in my embrace and I kiss her head and soothingly whisper 'Shhhh' over and over.

Looking to the officers, I recognize Cooper and Devon from when an officer was shot on the job. "Hey," we all say in unison.

"Can you tell me what's going on?" I ask.

Cooper steps to me. "Before we do, Flynn, can I ask your relationship to Baylor and Avery Evans?"

"Avery here is my girlfriend."

Ave nods in agreement and he explains what

happened. "It seems that Baylor was attacked at the apartment she shares with Avery, earlier this evening, by two unknown assailants. Avery here, interrupted them and probably saved her sister from getting kidnapped or worse."

"I was so scared, baby. I'm glad to be in your arms now," she says, as she tightens her arms around me, her body tight with tension.

"Avery was giving us all she can remember but she's in shock at the moment so her memories are vague."

"Ave lass, I'm so glad you weren't home when it happened." Placing a kiss on her head, I pull her back to look at me. "Do you know who they were?"

She shakes her head. "No, I don't think I've ever seen them before."

"Are they the guys from the other day?" She looks at me confused. "You mentioned two guys the other night?"

"I...I don't know. Everything's all so fuzzy." She sits down and rests her elbows on her knees and sighs.

Shaking my head, I run my fingers through my hair and I sit down next to her and rub her back. "What shit has your sister gotten into?"

Her head snaps toward me and the look she's currently giving me could turn me to stone. There's such vehemence in her gaze right now. "Who says it's her fault?" she snaps.

"I didn't say that, I—" Before I can defend myself, Clay enters the ER and walks toward us.

Standing up, I step away from Avery and over to Clay. "Clay, dude, how's Baylor?" I stretch out my hand to him.

"Flynn," he says, slapping me on the back with one hand and shaking the other in that manly one-hand shake/hug. "You know I can't discuss this with you, you're not technically family."

I nod my head in understanding but Avery says, "It's fine." As she slides her arm around my waist, snuggling into my side. I breath her in but she doesn't smell as florally as she usually does.

"Avery, it seems that Baylor was shocked with a Taser. There's two red barb welts on the side of her abdomen. She has a concussion. A small cut to her left cheek that needed five stitches, but luckily no broken facial bones. She has three cracked ribs and a nasty bump on the back of her head. Her face and ribs are bruised, likely from being kicked. All things considered, she's in okay shape."

"Jesus Christ," I mutter, rubbing my forehead.

Clay adds, "She's still unconscious and we will continue to monitor her until she wakes up."

Avery is frozen beside me. Rapidly blinking as she process his words. "Will...will she be okay?" she stammers.

"Until she regains consciousness, we won't know about her mental state but physically, yes, she will recover from these injures."

Avery nods her head and then falls into a chair. Looking up to Clay she asks, "Can I see her?"

Clay nods his head. "Of course. Come with me. Flynn, technically, you cannot see her."

Nodding my head, I say, "No, I understand." I turn to Avery. "You go see your sister, and I'll see about getting her transferred to a room upstairs."

She stands up, wraps her arms around me, and kisses me. There's something different about the kiss. There's no feeling or emotion that there normally is when we kiss. I put it down the to stress of what's happened with her sister. I watch as she follows Clay but something is niggling at me. Turning to Cooper and Devon, I fill them in on the recent issues with Baylor.

Wrapping up with the officers, I head back into the ER and stop at the nurses' station and arrange a room for Baylor. Five minutes later, they tell me there's a bed on four for Baylor and she'll be moved up in a few moments. Offering to tell Avery, I make my way to the cubicle Baylor is currently in.

Stopping outside I hear her say. "Please wake up. I'm so sorry, twinsie. Please wake up for me."

Hearing her words, I smile when I realize that even though they are going through a rough patch right now, she still cares for her sister and that only makes me love her more.

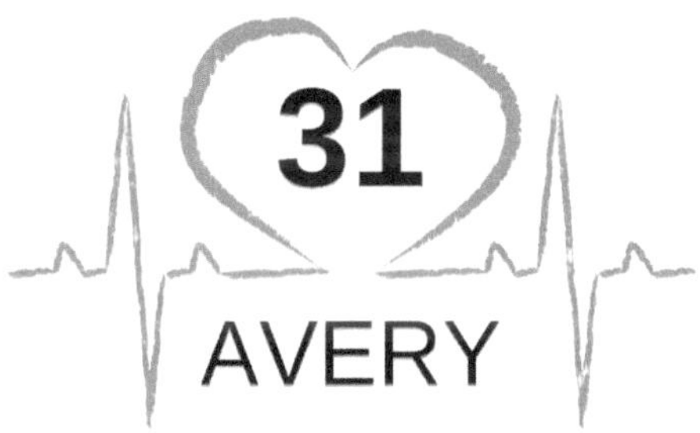

My body hurts.

My head aches.

Everything is fuzzy.

My eyes are heavy. I'm trying to open them but they refuse to move.

My body feels light, like I'm floating.

There's an incessant beeping that's grating through my brain. *Make it stop.*

Then I hear it, I hear him, Flynn, he's here but what he says confuses me.

"Ave lass, she'll be fine."

I'm not fine, I yell in my head.

Flynn, please help me. I plead, but he can't hear me. No one can hear me.

It's just me and my thoughts.

The beeping becomes louder and erratic.

There's a commotion around me, I can feel it happening but my eyes won't open for me to see. A warmth spreads over my body and I drift off into the blackness again.

I'm awake, again, and like before, everything is fuzzy.

My eyes still won't open.

My head now has a dull ache.

My body still hurts but not as much as before.

My throat is as dry as the Sahara and I need to pee really badly, then I realize I have a catheter in and reluctantly, I empty my bladder. *Eeeeew*, I think to myself as the 'Ahhhhhhhh' feeling of when you are peeing washes over me.

Laughing within my head, I try and open my eyes but like last time, my lids are heavy and weighted down. With all my might, I concentrate and my eyes flicker open. Blinking a few times, the room comes into focus. I'm in a hospital bed, huh? Confusion wraps around me.

"Avie," Bay says, leaning her head down, she grips my hand in hers and squeezes tightly. "I'm sorry you got caught up in this." I'm confused as to what she's saying. She grips my hand tighter but my lids start to droop. My body feels heavy, I can't keep them open. *No, Avery, stay awake*, I plead with myself, but the darkness wins and I doze off back into the black abyss.

I'm awake and just like the previous times, I will my eyes to open but they refuse to budge. Someone is holding my hand tightly, their grip is strong and comforting. There's a sound, I think it's a door opening. The grip on my hand disappears and I hear footsteps.

"Flynn, baby, what are you doing back here?"

What the hell?

"Just checking on my girl."

Flynn, I shout in my head. That's not me. Bay's doing it again. Flynn, I shout in my head over and over, my voice hoarse from screaming at him.

My eyes flit open and it looks like my sister and boyfriend just kissed. My heart rate spikes. My heart is rapidly beating within my chest, it hurts seeing my sister kiss him. It's beating faster and faster. The beeping is getting louder and louder. Panic is building within me.

I try to speak but I can't. My voice won't work, I'm willing myself to speak but my body and mouth don't want to cooperate.

Flynn steps around her—me—and races to my side, he'll be in doctor mode right now, it calms me that he's on my case. My heart rate slows down. My body relaxes. I try to speak but again, nothing comes out. My eyes are on his, I'm pleading with him to look at me, but he's focused on the monitors attached to me. The monitor starts to rapidly and loudly beep and I scream inside my head for him to look at me.

Flynn! Flynn! Flynn! I scream over and over.

The door flies open and a nurse comes racing in. I beg

and plead for her to look at me too but she and Flynn are chatting. Finally they turn to me but just as they do, my eyes close again. *Damn it,* neither of them saw me.

A warm feeling envelops my body from head to toe and once again I drift off into the darkness.

I'M WORRIED ABOUT AVERY. SHE SEEMS ON EDGE AND NOT just because her sister is in the hospital. She seems different but then again, I've never been with someone when a loved one is in the hospital. The doctor in me has always been reserved and watching from the outside, but this time, I'm a part of the inner circle and I don't like it much. I definitely prefer to be on the other side of things.

Avery's eyes keep darting around everywhere. I guess she keeps expecting the persons responsible for this attack to return. When I realise that's why, I stop overreacting.

Baylor woke for a few moments just before. Avery froze but as quickly as she woke, she drifted off again. I guess her body needs time to heal. She's been through a lot. She sure is one tough cookie, but then again, she is

Ave's twin, so they must be alike in that aspect. Leaving her with Baylor, I step out and walk toward the nurses' station. Avery needs someone to lean on so I call the one person I know she'd want here, Cressida.

Dialing her number, which I got from Preston, she picks up on the second ring. "Hey, this is Cress."

"Cressida, it's Flynn."

"Hey, Doc, and I've told you to call me Cress.

"Okay. Hi, Cress, it's Flynn."

"Much better," she teases, and I find myself grinning. "To what do I owe the pleasure of this call?"

"It's Avery—"

"What's wrong?" Her voice increases an octave when she says this.

"We are at Western General. Bay is here."

"Ohh shit. I'll get Mom to watch Lexi. Be there soon."

She hangs up and I let out a sigh. Turning around, I see Preston walking toward me. "Any change?" he asks.

Shaking my head, I reply, "Not really. She woke for a bit but was agitated so they sedated her again."

"Shit."

"Yeah. I just called Cress, she's on her way." His face lights up when I mention her name. "Thanks for her number by the way."

Before I can probe him regarding Ave's best friend, his pager beeps and saves him from my interrogation…for now. He looks at it. "Gotta run. Keep me posted."

Nodding, I say, "Will do."

Aimlessly, I wander the hospital. This not being

involved in the care of a patient is hard. I want to be there for Ave, but right now she's so lost in her head and worried about Baylor. Giving her time with her sister is the best for now, so I head own to the cafeteria.

Grabbing a coffee, I take a seat and mindlessly drink it. With the first sip, I scrunch my face up; I totally should have gone to the doctors' lounge and used the machine there, or better yet, to the shop across the road. My phone beeps with a text.

CRESS: *Just parked. Meet me in the ER.*
FLYNN: ***thumbs up emoji***

Grinning as I hit send because I know she hates emojis, Ave told me one day when they were texting back and forth. I thought Preston and I texting in gifs was bad, but if there was a team Olympic sport for texting, Cress and Avery would be the world champions.

Standing up, I pocket my phone, dump my coffee—if you could call it that—in the trash, and make my way back to the ER to meet Cress. She must be a speed walker because when I enter the waiting room, she's already here. She races over to me. "Flynn," she shouts. "How's our girl?"

"I don't know. She seems off. Doesn't seem herself."

"That's understandable."

"Yeah, I get that, but I don't know. I can't put my finger on it. I'm hoping you being here will put her at ease and pull her out of her funk."

"If I know Avery, she'll be putting on a brave front but on the inside, she'll be screaming and falling apart. She and Bay may not be in the best place right now but at the end of the day, Bay is her sister, and family means every-thing to Avery."

Nodding my head I agree with her. Avery is always there when you need her, and for her family. "Let's go then."

Cress and I head down the corridor and make our way up to Baylor's room. We step into the room and Cress immediately envelops Avery in a hug. "Ohh, Ave, I'm so sorry. Do you know why this happened?"

She shakes her head no, closes her eyes, and lets Cress comfort her but she seems stiff. Her face is ashen with worry. Stepping over to them, I wrap my arms around her from behind and kiss the side of her head. She lifts her arms and rubs her palms up my arms. Sighing deeply, she melts into me. *This is more like it*, I think to myself, *this is the Avery I know and love.* It's all starting to work out, that is until I look over at Cress, she looks concerned.

"Ummm," Cress says from where she's standing. "Flynn, can you get Ave some water, she looks parched and dehydrated."

Nodding, I whisper, "Be right back." Kissing the side of her head, I step out into the hall and stop when I see Preston hovering outside Baylor's room.

"Did I see Cress?" His eyes lighting up when he says her name. "She got here quickly."

"Yeah, she did. That woman can fly or something. She's really worried about Baylor but at the same time, she's mothering Avery, sending me to get her water."

"Well, she is a great mom. That instinct carries over in everything she does. How's Avery doing now?"

"Still the same. Still out of sorts."

"Can you blame her? Her sister was attacked outside their apartment. Any news from the police yet?"

"None yet. Until Bay regains consciousness, we won't know anything further."

From behind the door, I just exited I hear yelling. Preston and I eye each other and then we race over and open the door. Stepping into the room, I'm not prepared for what I hear.

I'M FLOATING, WELL, IT FEELS LIKE I'M FLOATING. MY BODY IS light yet heavy at the same time. There are raised voices nearby. I can't quite make out who they are, this fog in my head is making everything fuzzy and confusing. Add in the ache all over my body, and I can't make much sense of anything right now.

Fluttering my eyes, they open briefly before drooping closed again, but this time they don't feel like lead. I will them open and this time success, I blink rapidly. The room is blurry but it's starting to come into focus. My throat is dry and scratchy and when I try to speak, nothing comes out.

The fog clears and now everything is bright and my hearing is back, I don't understand what they are saying, it's like they are speaking a foreign language right now. I think it's Cress and she's angry, like momma bear angry. Then her words finally register. They play on repeat over and over in my head, "You're pretending to be her."

"Am not," someone who sounds like Baylor scoffs in reply.

"Please, you lying bitch." Yep, that's Cress. "The person lying in that bed is Avery Evans. Standing before me is bitchy Baylor Evans."

She's pretending to be me? Why? I'm confused right now.

"Baylor, why?" I scream but it's my mind because my eyes droop closed and once again, I begin to drift away from reality. *No! No! No!* I plead with my body but once again, it wins.

This time rather than drifting into darkness, it's gray and hazy and I feel like I'm floating.

You're pretending to be her. Am not.

You're pretending to be her. Am not.

You're pretending to be her. Am not.

This repeats over and over in my mind. What the fuck, Baylor? I'm so confused right now, surely what I'm hearing isn't what's happening. Panic begins to fester and in my mind I shout, *She's not me* over and over.

I'm pleading, *she's not me.*

My mind is crying. Pleading. Begging.

She's not me.

She's not me.

She's not me.

I keep chanting this as I will my eyes to open.

I will myself to speak.

I will myself to move, even a fraction, but my body won't cooperate. Anything, I just want my body to do something, but all I can do is lie here and listen to them bicker and argue.

"You are not her," Cress scoffs.

"Yes, I am!" Baylor yells back.

She's not me.

She's not me.

She's not me.

She's not me.

Come on body, do something.

I shout over and over in my mind.

She's not me.

She's not me.

She's not me.

She's not me.

Please body, do something. Anything. Please.

The door opens and Flynn snarls, "Enough!"

He's here, I think to myself. The atmosphere in the room freezes when he speaks. My eyes flicker open but no one is paying attention to me. Rage is enveloping the room and I'm forgotten about.

Please Flynn, look at me, I beg. Hoping he knows, hoping he feels my presence. Hoping our love is enough for him to see through her lies and deceit.

Flynn is talking.

The girls are yelling.

The voices begin to fade away and the last memory I have before I drift into the darkness is Flynn fighting for me.

I'm looking between Cress and Avery/Baylor/whomever arguing like children. My mind is racing to process what's playing out right now. My eyes drop to the person in the bed and then flick back to the doppelgänger standing next to me. I'm so confused , I don't know what's the truth or who to believe.

"You are not her," Cress scoffs, stepping toward Avery/Baylor, poking her in the chest.

My eyes look back and forth between the two of them as they continue to throw barbs at one another.

"Yes, I am!" Baylor/Avery yells back.

"You are not Avery Evans, I bet my life on it." Cress points at Baylor/Avery and she smacks her hand viciously away.

I've had it and I explode. "Enough!" I yell, they both jump at the loudness of my voice. Even I'm surprised at the forcefulness behind it. "Just stop it," I plead. "Whoever is in this bed needs rest. You two fighting like this isn't going to help." I shake my head and stare at the body lying in the bed. "Regardless of who this is," pointing to the bed, I go on, "you both need to show some respect. She was attacked, she doesn't need this in her recovery."

"Yeah, Cressida," Avery scoffs, and with that one comment, I start believing Cress that Baylor is parading around as Avery right now.

Stepping over to Avery/Baylor, Cress, reaches out and stops to me. "Flynn, that there Baylor Evans." I stare at her, then look to Avery/Baylor. I'm so fucking confused right now. "Flynn, the person in that bed is Avery. My best friend. Your girlfriend. I know it without an ounce of doubt." She pauses. "Flynn, I swear to you on my life. On Lexi's life, the person in that bed is Avery."

"Prove it," Baylor/Avery snarls, just as the door to the room slams open, hitting the wall with a thud. Security is here, probably from the yelling and commotion echoing out in the corridor.

"With pleasure," Cress snaps. "Yesterday morning, Avery and I got tattoos." My eyes scrunch in confusion, I knew they had brunch but this I did not know. Cress grabs the hem of her shirt and lifts it up. On her left hip is what looks like Lexi's handwriting, spelling out her name within a pink and blue inkblot. "I got this yesterday. Avery, the real Avery, got one on her wrist."

The woman beside me quickly hides her arms behind her back and her face drains of all color.

"Is this true?" I hesitantly ask, my voice laced with confusion and hurt.

"Flynn, babe, she's lying," Baylor/Avery whines.

"Show me your wrist!" I demand, my voice a few confused octaves higher than usual.

"No, I don't have to prove anything. I'm Avery. I'm your girlfriend. Flynn, please…" she pleads, but I don't believe her this time.

"Uhh, yeah, you do," Cress says, stepping toward Baylor but Preston, who I've just noticed is here, wraps his arms around her and pulls her back into him. He whispers something into her ear and she instantly deflates.

Walking to the bed, I pull back the blanket and lift Baylor/Avery's arm up. Sure enough, on her left wrist is a fresh tattoo. Holding Avery's hand, I squeeze and kiss her knuckles. Then the most amazing thing happens, her eyes flicker open and this time, after blinking rapidly, they stay open and focus on me. I'd recognize those gorgeous green orbs anywhere. When she realizes it's me, she smiles and it lights up her pale bruised face. "It's okay, lass, I'm here," I say, kissing her knuckles repeatedly. Relief floods through my body that she's regained consciousness.

"What's…what's going on?" she asks, her voice raspy and dry sounding.

"What do you remember?" I ask, doctor me takes over even though I want to wrap my arms around her and hug her dearly.

"It's all hazy." She pauses and thinks. "There were two men and then," a tear escapes, "one of them zapped me and then…and then…" She's a sobbing mess now and can't talk. Sitting on the bed, I lie down next to her and pull her into my arms. Her body is shaking. She flinches at my touch.

"I'm sorry, lass." Gently I place a kiss on her temple.

She nods. "I was so scared." She burrows into my chest and blubbers.

"Shhhh, you're safe now, lass. I won't let anything else happen to you," I say, running my fingers gently though her locks. "No one will hurt you again."

Turning my head, I look to Baylor, her face is ashen with fear and shock at being caught. Avery lifts her head from my chest and looks to her sister. "Why, Bay, why?" Avery sadly asks, her voice broken.

"I'm so sorry, Avie," Baylor says, stepping to the bed she reaches across me, offering her hand to her sister. In my arms Avery tenses, she hesitates to take her sister's hand.

The room falls quiet, until Cress breaks the silence. "Are you shitting us right now, Bay. Sorry, really? That's all you've got?" Cress scoffs, her disdain for Baylor shining brightly at this moment. "You better start talking now, bitch, and don't even think about lying to us."

"Shut it, Cressida," Baylor snaps, "No one asked for your opinion. No one wants you here. Go home to your bastard child. You aren't needed here."

Cress lunges for Bay but Preston pulls her back and stops her.

"That's enough!" I roar, jumping out of the bed I step to Baylor. I'm fuming right now. She freezes at my words and stares blankly at me. "Preston, can you please ask the officers to come into Avery's room? They need to speak to Baylor here."

"Sure, no worries," he says. "Glad you're awake, Avery." He turns to Cress. "Come on, Cress."

She rolls her eyes at him but when he stares her down, she relents. "Fine." Walking to the bed, she reaches out and squeezes Ave's hands. "I'll be right outside. I'm so mad at you right now, but I'm also glad you're okay." She bends down and kisses her on the cheek. She shoots a glare at Baylor and turns to face Preston. He places his hand low on her back and guides a reluctant Cress out of the room with him. The two of them walking precariously close together.

After the door closes, I look to Baylor sitting in the corner. "Baylor, you need to start talking and you need to tell us the truth. Do not think about leaving anything out or lying." She huffs, crosses her arms over her chest, and continues to sulk like a petulant child.

Avery and I look at one another. She winks at me and flinches as she does. I wink and she grins back at me. Taking a seat next to her, I lean over and kiss on her forehead, I whisper, "I'm so glad you're okay. I love you."

"Thanks. I love you too." Her gaze drifts over to Baylor. "Flynn, can you please leave me with my sister for a moment?"

"I'm not leaving you alone with her. She pretended to be you. Hell, she's probably the one who did this and she's blaming it on two innocent guys."

"Fuck you, Flynn," Baylor angrily shouts at me. "I'd never hurt my sister like that. Never."

"Not physically you wouldn't, but you did pretend to be her on several occasions. I don't trust you, the only reason I haven't kicked you out is because I want answers."

Avery cups my cheek in her palm. "Please, Flynn? I'll be fine. Bay won't hurt me."

"I don't like this but okay." I place another kiss on her forehead. "I'll be right outside this door."

Walking away from her is harder than I expected. Stepping into the hall, Cress and Preston walk over to me, his arm around her waist. "Everything all right?" Preston asks.

"Yeah. Ave wants to speak to Baylor."

"And you left her alone with that psycho bitch? I don't trust her," Cress says through gritted teeth. "One word and I'll take her skanky ho ass down."

"You've got a live one there, dude," I say, then they step apart and pretend like nothing is going on between them.

"Flynn, are you sure it's okay to leave them alone together?" Cress asks me again

Nodding my head, "Yeah, they'll be fine. I trust that Ave can handle her sister."

Cress nods and agrees. "If anyone can handle Bay, it's Avery. Look, I'm going to head to her place and grab a few things for her, I'll be back soon."

"Thanks, Cress."

My gaze drifts to the door that I just exited, and I hope with everything I have, I didn't just make a mistake leaving Ave alone with Baylor.

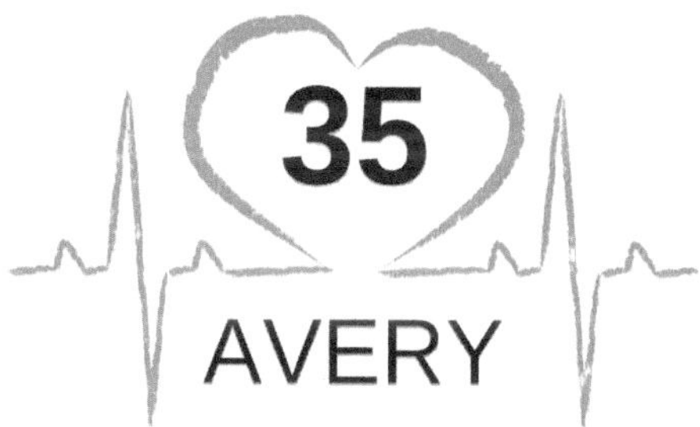

THE DOOR CLOSES BEHIND FLYNN AND BEFORE THE DOOR clicks shut I turn to Bay, and for the first time ever, I let loose on her. "Baylor Martine Evans, you are going to be straight with me and you are not going to lie." She tries to interrupt me, but I raise my hand and glare. She must sense that I'm more than pissed because she closes her mouth and stares at me. "For months now, you have not been yourself. You have turned into a big meanie head twatwaffle." This causes her lip to lift, mine too if I'm honest. "You have been horrible, absolutely horrible, to me and I want to know why?"

"Why what?" she snaps, crossing her arms defensively, like she always does when she knows she's in the wrong but doesn't want to admit it. She stares out the window at the darkening evening sky. I stare over at my sister and notice her shoulders are tight and high, she's hiding something. It frustrates me that she won't talk to me. Even though we're fighting right now, we've always talked to each other, and her not talking to me right now hurts more than the things she's done recently. "Why, Bay, why?" I plead again, but she continues to stare out the window. "Really, Bay, you're just going to ignore me?" Slapping my hand on the bed, I scoff in frustration when the silence becomes deafening. "What the fuck is going on, Bay?" I shout. Her head snaps to me and I just know the next thing out of her mouth will be more lies. Raising my hand, I stop her before she begins, "And don't you dare say nothing. Bay, you've been on a downward spiral for weeks now. You've become a horrible human being, I want my twinsie back. Hell, you pretended to be me—"

"We've done it before," she snaps.

"We were kids, Bay, AND if I remember correctly, Mom and Dad generally busted us." She eyes me. "Okay, they didn't always bust us, but we were kids. We did it for fun. This time, you tried to seduce my boyfriend AND when I was attacked, you pretended to be me." Pausing, I take a deep breath. I'm absolutely exhausted but I want the truth from her. "Please, Bay," I plead, "please talk to me."

She ignores me and I start to think she'll never open up and then she turns to face me; she lifts her gaze to mine and my heart breaks for my sister. Her eyes are full of despair and brimming with tears. She bites her lip worriedly. "Avie, I'm in trouble, big trouble and I don't know how to get out."

"Maybe I can help get you out. Please, Bay, just talk to me."

She shakes her head. "No, Avie, no one can. I...I've...I

got mixed up with these people and I started dealing for them." My eyes pop wide open at this revelation, my sister is a drug dealer. *What the hell?*

"Are you using?"

She vehemently shakes her head. "Nope. Never, you know I'd never touch them."

"But you'll sell them."

She sadly nods her head. "The high of doing a deal is exhilarating. It's the best, most euphoric feeling in the world. I became addicted to the high of doing deals. I'd never felt power, or euphoria like this before. I knew it was wrong…" *There's the Bay I know and love*, I think to myself. "…but I just couldn't stop, and then I got in way over my head. Kye—"

"That name seems familiar."

"He was another dealer and we became close. When he tried to get out…" She drifts off but I can guess what she's alluding to.

"He was killed," I answer for her. She sadly nods her head, a lone tear falls down her cheek, which she quickly wipes away.

"Ave, all this…" She flicks her hand around at me. "This happened," she sniffles, "because of me. You're in here because they thought you were me. This is all my fault." She drops to her knees and cries. She shuffles toward the bed and rests her head on the mattress and continues to cry. I sit here and watch my sister falls apart. The grief of what happened to me and losing her friend, Kye, is crushing her right now. And seeing her like this, it's crushing me too.

She lifts her head and looks at me. "I'm sorry, Avie," she sobs, she reaches out and squeezes my hands. "I'm so so sorry." Her body shudders as she lets it all out.

"Ohh, Bay," I say. Trying to sit up so I can console her, I flinch in pain. "Arrrgh," I moan, holding my ribs.

Bays head snaps up and when she sees me holding my side, she begins to cry again, harder this time. "Ohh, Avie, I'm so so sorry. Please don't hate me. I was so scared when I came home and saw what was happening. I didn't want them to hurt me too. I didn't know what to do. I panicked and pretended to be you to save my ass, but then it kinda spiraled. I was confused. I was scared. I was emotional. Once we got to the hospital, I kept up the facade. I don't know why I did that. Please forgive me."

"Bay, come here." I beckon her to me with my fingers. She takes my hand and sits on the edge of my bed. "I get why you pretended to be me while at the apartment, but I don't get why you did it here? Or why you pretended with Flynn the other week. I don't understand that."

"I don't know why I kept it up once we got here, but it was nice to feel wanted again. I'd pushed you away and after losing Kye, I was all alone and suddenly there were people everywhere and I was hugged, and I liked that. Had you not got a tattoo, totally badass by the way, I would have eventually been found out when you woke but for those few hours, it was nice being you. You really do have a great life and boyfriend."

"You can have it too, you just need to make a few changes. What about the other week when you went to Flynn's and pretended to be me? That wasn't to save your ass, that was to hurt me."

"I was in deep at that stage. I was hoping, if I split you and your Irish hottie up, you'd hide at home and be safe. I pretended to be you to save you."

"That was a seriously dumb plan."

She shrugs. "Hey, I'd popped a few pills beforehand. I

thought it was a brilliant plan. I didn't really know what I was doing."

My eyes pop open at her pill use declaration but then I remember her saying she hadn't used. "You just told me you didn't do drugs."

"Not the hard stuff. Pills are fine."

Shaking my head, I'm so disappointed in her right now. "I just…Bay, why? Why? I don't understand. You're a smart girl but this is really dumb."

"I don't know," she spits, "I was sick of living in your shadow. You're the angel twin. Great job, sweet school teacher. Me? I'm the college dropout. Always fucking up. Jumping from one shit job to the next. When this fell into my lap and it was something I was good at. I felt amazing for the first time in a long time."

"You're proud 'cause you're a drug dealer?"

"Never said I was perfect." She sighs deeply, "What am I going to do?"

"Tell the truth for starters. When the officers come back, you will tell them everything and suffer the consequences. It's time to grow up, Baylor Martine Evans."

"Wow, you used my full name again, twice in one day," she jokes and then swallows deeply. She looks at me. "I'm scared, Avie."

"And you should be, Bay." Pausing, I take a deep breath. "But I'll be here for you."

"Why?"

"You're my twin. I'd do anything for you." Reaching out I squeeze her hand and smile.

"You know if the shoe was on the other foot, I'd probably leave you at the mercy of the dealers, right?"

A laugh escapes me. "No, you wouldn't. You play tough, but underneath it all, you're just as sweet as me."

"It's a twin thing," we say in unison, and we both smirk at one another.

She squeezes my hand. "I really am sorry, Avie."

"I know."

There's a knock at the door and Flynn steps in with another doctor. "Ave lass, this is Clay, he just needs to check you over." He pauses and looks awkwardly at Baylor. "And, Baylor, the officers are outside wanting to speak to you."

She freezes next to me. "You can do this," I say, as I squeeze her hand reassuringly. She shocks me by standing up, leaning over, and hugging me.

"I love you, Avie," she sadly whispers.

"I love you too, BayBay," I say, as I hug her tightly back, using the childhood nickname I had for her. She laughs into my neck and holds me tighter; she's crushing me, and it kind of hurts but right now, she needs this. Pulling back, she looks to Flynn. "Let's do this," she says and I watch as my twin, for the first time in her life, faces up to her actions. I could not be more prouder of her, than I am at this moment.

My room is empty and the silence is nice. Lying back down, I stare at the ceiling and go over all that Bay told me. Sadness envelops me and I start to berate myself. I knew something was up, but I was so absorbed in my own life I didn't help her. I need to apologize to her next time I see her for not being there for her. Had I been, I don't think she'd be in the mess she is right now.

A few minutes later, Flynn walks back in and sits on the edge of my bed. "You okay?"

Staring up at the man I've fallen for, I nod. "As long I have you, I will be."

"I'm not going anywhere." He leans down and places

his lips against mine, but our loving moment is interrupted when Marvin comes barging in. "Where is she? And whose ass do I need to kick?" He pauses and looks to me. "Ohh, baby girl. What did they do to you? And why are there two of you?"

"Marvin," I say, happy to see my friend.

He walks over and takes a seat beside me. He looks me over from head to toe again. Reaching up, he cups my cheek, "What happened, baby girl?"

"It's a long story but I promise you, I'm fine."

"Okay, I trust you. But why am I seeing two of you? Did the quacks give me too much and I'm tripping right now?"

A laugh escapes me. "No, you're not tripping. That's my twin sister, Baylor. She's in trouble but we are going to fix it."

"Really?" Flynn questions, his voice laced with shock and apprehension.

"Yep. I'll fill you in later."

"Why do I always miss out on all the good stuff?" Marvin whines, but before I can reply, a nurse steps in, pauses, and crosses her arms.

At the same time, Marvin says, "Ohh oh, I'm in trouble."

And I say, "Ohh oh, you're in trouble." He and I both laugh, garnering ourselves an angry glare from the nurse.

"Marvin Marshall, you are going to be the death of me."

"You love me," he replies.

We all laugh at his candor. And if I'm honest, seeing him just now instantly relaxes me. I hope when I get to his age, I'm still this spritely. He says goodbye to me and promises to visit again tomorrow; shocking us all, he asks the nurse if it's okay.

Placing a kiss on my cheek, he and the nurse shuffle out and I watch as he exits. No sooner does the door close, it swings open and in walks Clay; I hadn't even noticed he had left. "Okay, Kelly," he points toward Flynn, "you need to get out so I can check on my patient."

Flynn nods his head, and I watch as the man I love leaves my hospital room, and I just know that everything from here on out will be smooth sailing.

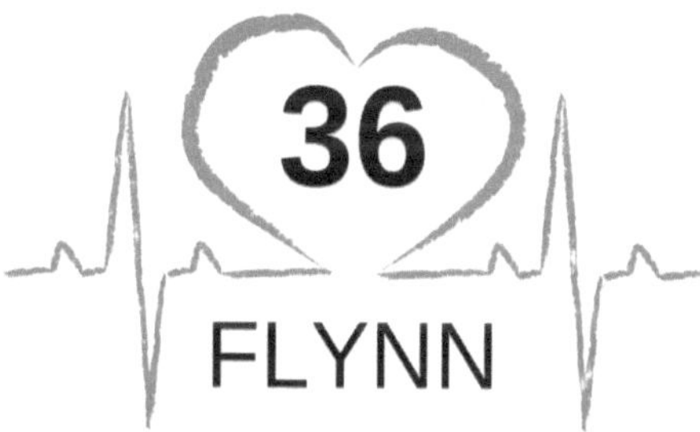

36

FLYNN

While I'm waiting, I lean against the wall by Avery's room. I'm so relieved she's okay. When it hit me it was her in the bed and not Baylor, I thought I was going to die. Seeing the woman I love unconscious is not anything I want to ever go through again. Someone stops next to me and I look up to see Baylor.

"Flynn—"

"No. I don't have anything to say to you."

"That's fair."

We stand here staring at one another. "Actually, I do have one question. Why? Why would you do that to your sister? Your flesh and blood?"

She shocks me when she starts to cry. Shaking her head from side to side, she wipes at the avalanche of tears. "I'm sorry." She blubbers, "Avie knows everything and her forgiveness is all I care about, but I would like to be civil with you, for her. And in order to do that, I need to apologize to you."

"I'm listening." Crossing my arms, I lean back against the wall and wait. She doesn't speak and when I look to her, she's looking at her feet. "Baylor," she looks up at me and I see remorse written all over her face.

"Flynn, I'm so sorry I deceived you the way that I did. I didn't mean to let it go on as long as I did. When I stepped out of the elevator and saw those two guys with Avie, I panicked. Everything happened so fast and then it just snowballed from there. I wanted to come clean so many times over the last few hours but I'm scared."

"Scared of what?"

"Them coming back."

"What did the police say?"

"Not much. I hope when I go and see them to give my formal statement, that they'll have more." She steps to me and places her hand on my forearm and squeezes, for a small chick, she's mighty strong. "You need to keep her safe."

"With my life." And I mean that, I would lay my life down to save Avery, in a heartbeat.

"Thank you." She swallows deeply and removes her hand. She brushes her hair behind her ear and it reminds me so much of Ave. "You know, you really are the perfect person for Avie. You are the complete opposite to her, but they say opposites attract. You've brought out a side to my sister that I didn't know existed. I kinda like her sassy, strong side. You two are clearly attracted to one another. You can feel the love radiating from you both when you're together, and I don't think I've ever seen Avie this happy before." She pauses, and sighs. "With my recent antics, I'm glad she has you by her side."

"Even though you tried to break us up."

"Semantics but, Flynn," we stare at each other and an understanding passes between us. "You hurt her and I will fucking kill you."

With that, she turns around and walks away from me. Maybe I've misjudged Baylor, I think she's just lost. With Ave and me on her side, we'll help her get back on the right track.

Clay exits Avery's room. "All good?"

"You know I can't tell you anything." I eyeball him. "Fine, but if I get fired I'm taking you down with me."

"Fine, but she's going to be my fiancée one day so…"

"Really?"

"Yep, now, how is she?"

"She's fine, considering. No lasting damage, but she will be sore for the next few days. I'm going to keep her in for another night and she can go home tomorrow."

"Can't I take her home and watch over her? I am a doctor, you know."

"No, you can't. And don't even think about playing the doctor card."

"Fine," I relent. Offering my hand, he takes it and shakes. "Thanks, man, appreciate you taking such good care of my girl."

"Never thought I'd see the day when Flynn Kelly was smitten with a woman."

"You've met her, it's hard to not fall for her."

"I agree…just don't tell my wife that."

We both laugh. He walks down the corridor and I head back into Ave's room. Pushing the door open, the room is dark, except for the night light above her bed. Avery's eyes are closed. I take a moment to look at her. Even with a messed-up face, she really is the most beautiful woman in the world.

"Stop staring at me, you creeper," she says with her eyes still closed.

"I'm just admiring your beauty."

"I think you need your eyes tested. I feel like shit and I'm pretty sure I look like a zombie right now."

"A sexy as fuck zombie," I say, as I step toward her. "And I love you just the way you are."

"Did you just Bruno Mars me?"

"Guess I did, but it's the truth. Avery, you are the most stunning woman in the world, zombie look included, and I'm the luckiest man alive to have you as my girlfriend."

"You say the sweetest things, Flynn Kelly, now come over here so I can kiss you."

"You had me at kiss."

Bending down, I gently grip her jaw in my fingers and press my lips to hers. It's a soft and gentle kiss, but it's the most perfect kiss ever in the history of kisses. Against her lips I murmur, "I love you, Avery Evans."

"I love you too, Flynn Kelly." She pulls back, her eyes darken with desire. "Wanna quickie?"

A deep laugh breaks free, shaking my head I run my finger over her bottom lip. "Avery, I would love nothing more than to fuck you all night long, but not three hours ago you were unconscious. Your body needs rest." She pouts. "But I promise, as soon as you are one-hundred-percent, I will eat you, suck you, and fuck you repeatedly. All.Night.Long."

"You know, you said that to me in the alcove the night we met."

"I did not know this but I can unequivocally say, that was the best night of my life...it led me to you."

"I agree one-million-percent with that statement. Now get out of here, so I can sleep and heal because I can't wait to fuck you repeatedly, all night long."

"Fiend," I playfully reply.

"Takes one to know one."

After kissing her longer than necessary for a goodbye, I leave her and head home. I'm exhausted. The events of last night and today have caught up with me. Hopefully, it's all smooth sailing from here.

"You okay? Do you need anything? Do you want me to call Flynn? What can I do?" She says all of this in one breath.

Shaking my head side to side. "No, I'm all good. What are you doing here?"

"I didn't want you to be alone so I came back. You looked so peaceful when I got here, I was going to climb in with you like we did in the past, but I wasn't sure if I'd be welcome." A tear breaks free. "Avie, I cannot express how sorry I am for what I've done recently."

Reaching out my hand, I flick my fingers at her. She jumps up and takes my hand in hers and sits next to me. "BayBay, you are my sister and I will always be here for you...even when you do stupid shit."

"You are the best sister ever."

"I know. Now you know what will make *you* the best sister?"

"What?" She wipes her nose on her shoulder sleeve and I shudder.

"That's gross, Bay."

"Whatevs. Now, what will get me into the best sister book?"

"Coffee."

"Huh?"

"Let's go to the cafeteria and get coffee."

"I'd like that."

Bay helps me slip my robe on—thank you Cress for bringing me a bag—and then she bends down to assist with my Birkenstocks. Once I'm dressed, as such, we link arms and head down to the cafeteria.

Since it's early, and we are the only ones here, we get our coffees quickly and take a seat. We each take a sip and spit it back into the cup. "Oh My God, that tastes—"

"Like shit...actually, it's worse than shit." We both laugh. "Ave, there's a Starbucks across the road, feel like a walk?"

Looking down at what I'm wearing, I hesitate but I really need coffee. "Fuck it. Sure, let's go."

Linking arms again, we head across the road and fifteen minutes later we each have a grande coffee in hand and contented looks on our faces. "Much better."

"Much."

We decide to head back to the hospital grounds, since I'm not really dressed for public viewing. I wave at Clay as we cross the road, he does a double take when he sees us. "Damn, I must be tired, I'm seeing two."

"Clay, this is my twin, Bay. Bay, this is Clay."

"We met," he growls.

"Nice to officially meet you," Bay offers. "I'm sorry about yesterday."

Before this awkward encounter can get any more awkward, Clay's pager goes off and he leaves us to race back to the hospital. I can feel Bay pulling away and retreating into herself. "Stop it, Bay."

"I'm not doing anything."

"Do I look dumb?" She goes to say something snarky and I bump her shoulder. "Don't let others' opinions or feelings affect you. Yes, you made mistakes but those who matter, as in me, are the only people's opinions you need to worry about. Now, get me back to my bed, I need to rest. This was a huge outing."

Bay nods and we continue our walk back to the hospital. A van comes screeching into the driveway. Just before we reach the doors, a man jumps out, shoves me to the ground, grabs Bay, and drags her into the vehicle, her kicking and screaming. She's fighting her assailant, but he's bigger and stronger. He throws her into the car, slams the door shut, climbs back in, and they drive off.

It all happens so quickly, I don't have a chance to call for help or do anything.

"Baylor!" I scream at the retreating van. Tears begin to well in my eyes. "Baylor!" I shout again but it's no use, the van is gone. Security rushes over to me and I look up at them. "My sister, they took my sister."

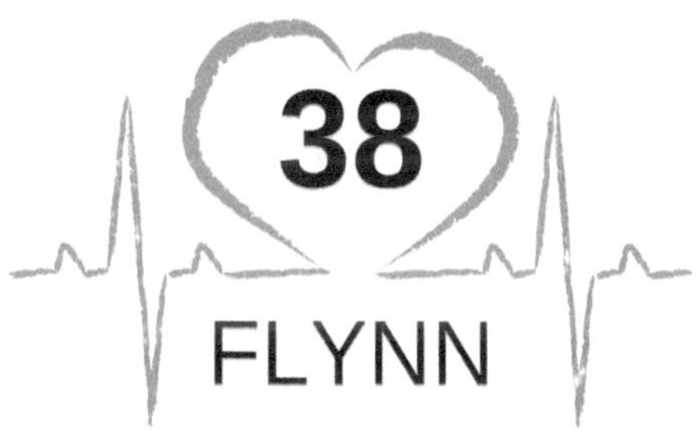

"FLYNN," SHE BLUBBERS

"Ave lass, what's wrong?"

"They…they took Bay," she cries, and the heartache in her voice crushes me.

"Who took Bay?"

"The guys. They finally got her. Flynn, they…they took her." She sniffs, "Flynn, I need you."

"I'm on my way."

"Thank you. Please hurry."

"I love you, Avery. And I'm sure Bay will be fine, if she's anything like you, which I suspect she might be, she'll be okay."

"I hope you're right, Flynn."

Me too. "I'll be there soon."

Hanging up, I quickly change and race to the hospital. When I arrive at Western General, the place is swarming with police. An officer is looking over my credentials when I hear my name being yelled. Looking up I see a disheveled Avery running toward me. "Flynn," she wails as she throws herself at me. My arms wrap around her and she breaks down and cries into my neck.

"Shhhh," I whisper, "I'm here now."

She loosens her grip on me. "Flynn, they still haven't found her. They took BayBay."

"Lass, give them time. It's only been an hour."

"But—" Pressing my finger to her lips I shush her. "No buts, give them time. Now, let's get you back to your room. This won't be good for your recovery; you are still fragile yourself. You need to get strong so you're better when she gets back."

"But Bay needs me to be out looking for her."

"Ave lass, no. You can't go looking for her. Those guys have already attacked you once, I won't let them attack you again. Bay would want you to be safe."

"But I need to find her, Flynn. I need my twinsie back."

"She will be back before you know it. Now, back to bed. Let's go."

We walk inside and are immediately met with Marvin. "No need to call the popo, I was just in the nursery."

"If I thought that would work, I would call them but I'm pretty sure you'd evade them too," Helen says. "Can't wait until you are back at the home."

"You'll miss me," he teases.

"Yeah, like a hole in the head. What's going on here?" Helen questions.

"Ave's sister was taken."

"You okay, babycakes?" Marvin asks her, shoving me aside and wrapping her in a hug.

"When Bay is back I will be."

"How about I hang with you for a few hours…as long as that's okay with my keeper?"

"Do you promise to stay with Avery and not wander off?"

"Cross my heart, hope to die. Stick a needle in my eye."

"You leave her room and I might just do that. I'll come collect you just before lunch."

"Thank you, Helen," he says, his tone super cheeky. Helen shakes her head as she walks away. "Come on, let's get you into bed." He says this with a suggestive eyebrow shrug. Ave and I both laugh, but we follow him back to her room.

Avery does as she's told and climbs into bed. Marvin takes the chair by the window and I climb on to the bed with her.

"Young love, it's so nice to see," Marvin says. "Now, what are we gonna watch while we wait for your sister to be rescued?"

"Your choice," Ave says, her voice quiet. I can tell she's shrinking into her head again and just as I think that, her body shakes in my arms, she's crying again.

"Ohh, Avie," I say, this causes her to cry harder.

"Bay is the only one who…who calls me Avie," she blubbers; pushing her head into my shoulder, letting it all out.

"I'm so sorry, Ave."

"It's not your fault. It's those guys' fault." She lifts her head. "What if I don't get her back? I don't know how to exist without her."

"She'll be fine."

"Doc's right," Marvin agrees, "If she's half the woman you are, then those fools are in for a treat. She'll be back before lunch."

But Marvin wasn't right, it's now been three days since Baylor was taken and she's still yet to be found. It's like she disappeared off the face of the Earth. Avery is beside herself with worry right now, and I'm worried about her. If we don't find Bay soon, I don't know how Avery is going to cope.

SHE'S BEEN GONE FOR FOUR DAYS NOW. NINETY-SIX HOURS and there's still no sign of my sister. I'm going out of my mind. I'm sick to death of hearing people say, "Everything will be fine" or "Bay is tough." I know she's tough, but my mind is racing right now. One minute I'm calm and think yes, she'll be home soon, and the next, I'm screaming and crying with fear that she's dead. I'm on an emotional roller coaster right now. Everyone is hovering around me like I'm going to fall apart at any second, I'm fine…ish, apart from wanting my sister back. I want some space. I just want to be left alone and with Flynn heading into work today, I might just get some peace. But noooo, I can't be trusted on my own so I agreed to go to the hospital with him. I'll hang with Marvin for the day.

I've been here for three hours and Marvin has kept me entertained, and my mind off Bay. He's just drifted off to sleep, so I take the opportunity to get some alone time. I head across the road to Starbucks since the coffee in the cafeteria here is toxic waste. With my coffee in hand, I'm walking back to the hospital when two men in suits approach me. "Avery Evans?"

Hesitantly, I really. "Yeeees. And you are?"

"I'm Agent Hall and this is my partner, Agent Oates." My eyes pop open at this, and I giggle. They both look at me in a 'yes we know our names are funny' way. They are talking but I'm not listening, I'm singing "I Can't Go for That (No Can Do)" by Hall & Oates to myself. It isn't until Hall, I think, says, "Ma'am, can you come with us, please?"

"Is this about my sister?"

"We aren't any liberty to discuss that here with you."

"Just tell me if she's okay."

A look passes between the agents. "Yes," one of them sternly answers. With that one word, I can finally breathe easily again. "Avery, if you come with us, we can tell you more."

"Can I let my boyfriend know what's happening?"

"No, not right now. Time is of the essence here, Ms. Evans."

"Fine, I'll come...but I'm texting him as soon as we leave."

"Fine."

"Actually, can you show me ID before I get in a car with you? Stranger danger and all that shit."

They both show me their identification, and much to their amazement, I quickly grab a snapshot of Hall's. Thank you, Cress, for teaching me the art of the quick sneaky pic. "For security," I say and I quickly send it to Flynn.

> **AVERY -** *Going with Agents Hall and Oates, yes that's their names. It's about Bay. Call you soon **attach ID picture***

No sooner do I send the message and my phone starts to ring. I answer but before I can say anything, Flynn bellows down the line, "Are you fucking crazy going off with strangers?"

"They aren't strangers. They are agents, Hall and Oates, and they have information on Bay."

"You are making me fucking crazy."

"It's about Bay and I'll be fine. Besides, you have a pic of Hall's ID. If this was a setup, they would have taken me like they did Bay, rather than talk to me and ask me to come with them." Just as I say this, the police station comes into view. "Look, we've just arrived at the station, see I'm fine. I'll call you as soon as I'm done here."

"You better. Please be safe and remember I love you."

"I love you too."

Hanging up, I sigh. Suddenly I'm nervous. "Is Bay here?"

They ignore me and quietly we walk into the station. They take me into an interrogation room and when the door opens, my eyes well with tears. "BayBay," I blubber as I take her in. Her clothes are torn, her hair's a mess, and her face—her gorgeous face—is black and blue and swollen. Racing over to her, I wrap my arms around her and she returns the gesture.

Together we cry with relief at seeing one another.

Pulling back, I gently grip her cheeks in mine. "Are you okay?"

She nods. "Yeah, I am."

"What happened?"

"Long story."

"Bay," I warn.

"I'll tell you, but first, I need you to sit and listen to what I have to say."

I sinking feeling develops in my stomach. I've never seen Bay like this before. "I'm not going to like this, am I?"

She shakes her head. "Probably not, but, Avery, I need to do this. I need to make amends for my actions." She swallows deeply. "I need to do this for Kye."

"Who is Kye, Bay?"

She sniffs. "He was 'the one' and because of my actions, he died. It should have been me but he protected me. I tried to walk away after that but I was in too deep. Way too deep." She licks her lips and looks at me. "Avie, this is my chance to put things right. This is my chance to make up for his death."

"I'm so proud of you, BayBay." And that's the honest truth. Last week, I was broken up and hurt over my sister but this week, I could not be prouder of her. This the Bay I know and love. She's taking charge and trying to put things right. "Okay, now, tell me the plan."

Taking a seat next to her, she tells me what's happened over the last four days. My sister is one tough chick, not many people would have survived what she went through. Then she tells me what's going to happen next; I'm a mix of unease and pride. For the next several hours, I'm brought up to speed on what's going to happen now. The more I'm told, the more I don't like it. To say I'm scared is the understatement of the century. I'm beyond frightened for my sister right now, but everyone assures me it will all work out and Bay will be safe.

I'm scared shitless with regards to what she's about to embark upon, but at the same time, I'm one extremely proud sister.

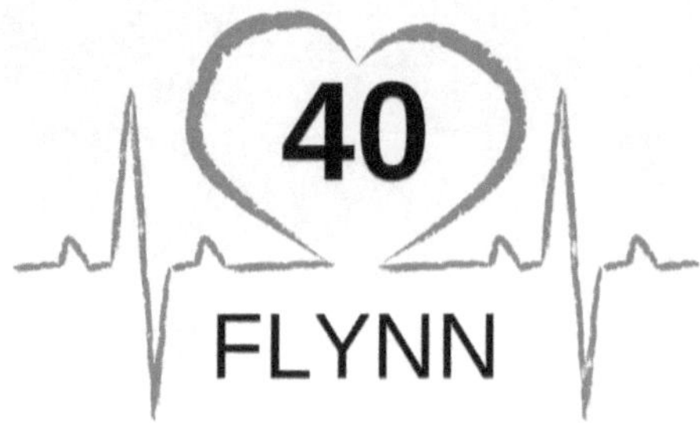

THE LAST FEW WEEKS HAVE BEEN CRAZY, MY LIFE FEELS LIKE something from the movies. I've had identity swapping, mistaken identity, an attack on Avery, kidnapping, undercover work, but there's also been happiness, joy, and love. Avery and I are hopelessly in love and we are happier than ever. As much as she's putting on a brave face, I know she's worried about Bay. Bay going undercover was a shock but at the same time, it's not a surprise. She likes living on the wild side, and if I'm honest, I'm impressed with the turnabout in Avery's sister.

Life is simply perfect at the moment, and this weekend, I'm going to whisk my girl away for the dirty relaxing weekend we need and deserve. Looking up from the chart I'm finishing up, I see Helen walking toward me and smirk, clearly Marvin has gone AWOL; again. "Has our resident Houdini escaped again?"

She shakes her head and as she steps closer to me, I see devastation written all over her face. I know what she's about tell me isn't good news; so much for our perfect life right now. "No, but I wish he had." She swallows deeply. "Marvin passed about an hour ago."

Standing up, I walk over to Helen and wrap my arms around her. She hiccups a sob and breaks down in my arms. "I'm going to miss the old coot," she blubbers.

"I think we all will. The hospital just won't be the same without him here."

"I know," she sniffles and steps back, wiping the tears from under her eyes. Our moment is interrupted by a beautiful angelic voice that breaks the silence. "Hey, guys."

Helen and I both snap our heads toward Avery and without saying anything, her face drops. She knows. Her eyes well and she shakes her head from side to side as the tears break free. She drops to her knees and breaks down. "No, no, no. He can't be gone."

Helen squats down next to Ave. "Avery, honey, he's in a better place now. You know how much pain he was in these last few days."

"I know, but he's gone and I didn't get to say goodbye."

"Avery, he knew how much you cared. Since he met you, he changed. You gave him the best possible last few weeks anyone could have asked for. He loved you like a daughter."

"I know but…" She shakes her head sadly. "He wasn't just my friend, he was my family." She looks up at me and my heart breaks when I see the devastation on her face. "Flynn, Marvin's gone."

Dropping to my knees, I pull her into my chest. She lets out all her grief over the loss of her friend.

We have just returned to Avery's apartment after Marvin's funeral, today was tough, but it was also good for her, it allowed her to say her goodbyes to Marvin. As we were leaving, the funeral director gave me an envelope for Avery. I'm unsure as to when to give it to her. She's an emotional wreck right now. I'm glad that Bay and Cress are here for her. Bay can't be as much as she'd like, due to her predicament, but Ave is pushing everyone away at the moment.

Ave heads into her bedroom and I stand in the living room, unsure of what to do. Removing my suit jacket, the envelop falls out, just as Avery steps back into the room. She bends down, picks it up, and looks at it. Her eyes widen when she sees her name scrawled on the front.

"What's this?"

"The funeral director gave it to me to give to you."

"Who's it from?"

Shrugging my shoulders, I admit, "I don't know. You'll need to open it to find out."

She swallows deeply and stares at the envelope. "Will you stay with me while I do?"

"Of course I will. I'm here for you anytime you need me."

She sadly smiles before taking my hand and pulling me to the sofa. She sits down and I sit next to her. She slides her finger under the flap, tears it open, and pulls out the letter. She begins to read and tears well in her eyes.

My dear Avery,

You reading this means I'm up in heaven with my harem of angels, running amok and finally living pain free. You were the light that kept me going these last few months. Your friendship meant everything to me. Thank you for keeping this old geezer smiling in my last days. Please don't dwell on my passing, live for the both of us. Focus on Flynn, name your little boy Marvin, after me, and keep that evil doppelgänger sister of yours in line.

Avery, you have the biggest heart and I'm so glad to have known you. If I had a daughter, I hope she'd be like you. Don't ever let anyone dull your shine, continue to sparkle each and every day.

Cheers,

Marvin

"Ohh, Marvin," she says, wiping away her tears. She looks to me and sadly smiles. "He was the sweetest man. I'm going to miss him so much, Flynn."

Placing a kiss on her temple, I pull her into me. "He sure was. Will you be okay, lass?"

"Yeah, I will be," she says. "Can you take me to bed and snuggle with me? I just want to be held."

"Anything you need and I'll do it."

We walk into her room and strip out of our clothes. We climb under the covers and snuggle, her back to my front, just like she wanted. "Marvin wants us to name our son Marvin."

"Marvin Kelly, I like it."

"Marvin Evans has a good ring to it too."

"Dr. Evans, I like it."

She rolls over to face me. "You'd change your name for me?"

I nod my head. "Yep, whatever it takes to have you in my life is what I'll do."

"You continually amaze me, Flynn Kelly, but it will be me who changes my name, it's tradition."

"Your strength continues to astound me, and I thank the heavens every day for allowing me to meet and fall in love with you."

"And I love you too. Now make love to me, Flynn. Show me how much you really do love me."

And that's exactly what I do. For the rest of the afternoon and evening, Avery and I make love until we blissfully fall asleep wrapped in each other's arms.

AVERY

...six months later

AFTER THE INCIDENT OF MISTAKEN IDENTITY, ENDING UP IN hospital, Bay's kidnapping, and the undercover sting thing, everything changed. The day Agents Hall and Oates —I still laugh at that—came to get me from the hospital, my world was turned upside down. After Baylor was rescued from B1 and B2—Bozo one and Bozo two—she was arrested for her part in the drug racket, but she offered to go undercover to help them bring down the biggest party drug operation in the state. Her offering this reduced her overall jail sentence. Had she not been arrested when she was twenty, her sentence could have wholly been suspended, but a dumb drunken night and a stolen garden gnome changed that for her. Luckily for Bay, B1 and B2 were killed when's she was rescued. They were high as kites and stood no chance against the team that was sent it. Their deaths, however, helped Bay in more ways than one. With no one to dispute her story, it played into the undercover setup and sting. Bay used them as her scapegoat with the drug leaders. They were impressed with her tenacity and she quickly worked her way into the inner ranks of the chain. Little did they know, she was gathering as much evidence as possible to bring them down.

The day it all went down, it made headline news. Bay and I hadn't spoken in a few days, so I was antsy and on edge. When it hit the news, and I knew she was safe; I could finally relax. The three months it took was nerve-wracking but with Flynn by my side, I was able to cope.

I'm so proud of my sister, but when it was all over, it was time for her to head to jail and serve out her twelve-month prison term. She's been inside for three months now and without her at the apartment, I'm lonely. I miss her like crazy, we've always been together—twin thing—so it's weird to not see her each and every day. I visit her every weekend, if Flynn isn't working, or sleeping, he comes with me since I'm generally at his place anyway. I spend most of my nights at his penthouse, basically we are unofficially living together.

Last weekend, when I went to visit Bay, Flynn had to work and it was just me. After a lengthy discussion, and a few raised voices, Bay and I decided to give up our apartment, as long as Flynn would officially let me move in.

That afternoon, I was excitedly awaiting him to get home from work. I baked to keep my mind occupied and I also cooked a lasagne big enough to feed the hospital. He stepped through the door and my excitement bubbled over. As usual, he went and had a shower to freshen up. I was a bundle of nerves while I waited so I opened a bottle of red, and I was on glass number two when he emerged, freshly showered and looking mighty sexy.

Handing him a glass, I top up mine and we head outside to watch the sunset from the patio. We are snuggling on the outdoor lounger, one of my favorite things to do. Looking up, at him, I take a deep breath and broach the moving in topic. "So, um, babe, today Baylor and I decided to give up our apartment."

His head snaps in my direction. "Okay, but where are you going to live?"

"Well, I was kinda sorta hoping you'd let me move in here…with you!"

He stares at me. Not saying a word. The silence is deafening. I start to think he doesn't like the idea of us officially living together when his lip lifts and he breaks into the biggest smile ever. "Does this mean that officially you'd be waking up naked in my arms each and every morning?" Nodding my head, I open my mouth to agree, but he raises his hand and presses his finger to my lips to stop me. "So three hundred and sixty-five days of the year, you will be waking up naked in my arms?"

"Yep," I say letting the 'p' pop.

"Best.Fucking.Day.Ever," he declares.

He takes my glass from my hand and places both glasses on the deck, he then pulls me into his arms and presses his lips to mine. Then I'm flying through the air and I'm thrown over his shoulder. My head has the perfect view of his denim-clad ass as he stalks back inside. He takes me into the bedroom, strips me naked, and gently pushes me back. Falling to the mattress, I stare up at my sexy doctor boyfriend as he begins to strip off his clothes. I'm excited for what's about to transpire, but he shocks me when rather than fucking me, he climbs onto the bed next to me. He pulls me into his arms and we snuggle together naked. We drift off to sleep, wrapped in each other's embrace.

The next morning, I wake naked in his arms, just like Flynn predicted. Rolling to my side, I smile when I realize he's already awake. "Good morning," I huskily say, my voice still sleepy.

"I love waking up like this."

"Me too." Lifting my hand, I cup his cheek in my palm and run my finger along his jaw. The stubble tickling me.

"I love you, Avery Evans, and I cannot wait for this to be official official."

"Define official official?"

"Your stuff here. You redecorating this place to turn it from a drab bachelor pad penthouse to OUR love nest penthouse."

"Really? I can add a few feminine touches?"

He nods at me. "Yep, this will be your home too, Avery. I want you to be comfortable here."

"As long as I have you, that's all the matters."

He leans forward and presses a kiss to my lips and then FINALLY, I get lucky.

Sure it's crazy to be moving in together, considering I've only known Flynn for less than a year but when you know, you know. And it feels right, so we are taking the plunge and have decided to officially cohabitate together. Some say it's too soon—I'm looking at you, Cress—but we don't care what anyone else thinks. We are happy with our decision, and that's all that matters. Truth be told, from the moment my eyes landed on the sexy as sin Irish doctor at the Tavern, I started falling so this was inevitable.

...later that day

Flynn didn't waste any time and he rallied the troops and today is officially the day I move in with him. With Baylor incarcerated, it was up to me to move us out, but thankfully, with the help of Preston, Cress, Lexi, and Flynn it wasn't as daunting as I expected, packing up two people's lives. Bay and I had lived here for nearly seven years. We had accumulated a lot of crap in that time. Bay's stuff was placed in storage and my things were transferred to Flynn's, well I guess, our place.

Never in my wildest dreams did I think I'd be living in a penthouse apartment, or be hopelessly in love, but here I am doing both. I am irrevocably in love with Flynn Kelly, and today I moved in with him. Oh My God, I'm your cliché love song right now—cue sappy love song music—but I don't care. I'm the happiest I've been in a long time.

After a grueling day, Preston, Cress and Lexi have just left...together. I cannot wait to have drinks with Cress soon to grab all the gritty, sexy gossip on her and a certain pediatric doctor because there is definitely some, okay a lot, of sexual tension between the two of them. It's been going on for months now, but my best friend is playing coy. The fact he's amazing with Lexi confirms my suspicion that something is going on between them, AND Lexi is extremely friendly with him. It's like they already know one another, because it usually takes Lexi time to warm up to people, especially men due to her douche hat father, but she and Preston are buddies already.

Flynn has taken the last box down to the car and I

stand in the now empty apartment. Looking around, I sadly smile. Baylor and I had some great times here over the last seven years. It was here that I got my acceptance letter to college, had my graduation party, celebrated my placement at Westside Elementary, AND it was the place where Flynn and I first confessed our love for one another.

Closing my eyes, a smile appears on my face when I feel Flynn's presence behind me. He wraps his arms around my waist and pulls me back into his chest. He nuzzles my ear and whispers, "I love you, Avery Evans, and I cannot wait to live with you."

Spinning in his arms, I drape mine over his shoulders and gaze into his sparking blue eyes. "I love you too, Dr. Kelly, now take me home and ravish me."

"Home, I like that."

"Yeah, me too…now let's go."

"With pleasure, Ms. Evans, with pleasure."

An hour later, we are standing in the kitchen by the island counter. Flynn is in a pair of denim jeans which sit low on his hips. I'm wearing my pale pink satin sleep shorts, with matching cami top, and my beige slouchy cardigan, as there is a chill in the air tonight.

Flynn opens a bottle of red and pours us each a glass. He hands one to me and when our fingers brush, a sizzling zing zaps through my body, causing me to shiver.

"You cold, Ave lass?"

Shaking my head, I smile at him. "No, I'm good."

"You are more than good, you look sexy as fuck in this." His eyes roam over me and my body temperature rises, causing me to shiver again. He takes my wine glass from me and before he places it next to his on the counter-top, he takes a sip. Leaning forward, he nuzzles along my jaw. "Mmmmm, wine tastes so much better with a side of Avery."

He steps back, resting against the counter, and we stare at one another. The air around is pings with lust, desire, and everything in between. Picking up my glass, I take a sip, place it down, and pressing my lips against his for a quick kiss.

Pulling back, I stare at him and nod, "Personally, I think this wine is better with a side of Flynn."

"Agree to disagree?" he counters.

Stepping to Flynn, I cup his cheek in my palm. "Agree to disagree." I run my thumb along his chin and stare into his baby blues. His scruff is longer than usual and I wonder what it will feel like between my thighs. My cheeks heat at this dirty thought and I smirk.

"What are you smirking at?" Lifting my gaze to his, my cheeks darken further and he smiles back at me. "You little minx, you. Tell me what dirty thoughts you have?"

"Who says they are dirty?"

"You did. Your cheeks are currently dirty pink and your breathing in labored. Now, tell me?"

He rests one hand on my hips and the other on the countertop edge. Leaning back an inch, he stares intently at me. My insides quiver at the intensity of his gaze. Rubbing his cheek, I tell him what I was thinking.

"I like the way you think dirty, Avery. Now kiss me and I might make your thoughts a reality."

Closing my eyes, I lean in and press my lips ever so softly to his. Our kiss starts out soft and gentle, but it quickly turns heated. Without warning, I'm flying through the air and then I'm sitting on the edge of the countertop. Flynn quickly pulls down my sleep shorts and panties. His gaze flicks from my face to between my thighs. Spreading my legs wide, I raise my eyebrows seductively at him. His face widens in a sexy grin and he gently pushes me back so I'm lying on the countertop. He drops to his knees in front of me. With his eyes locked on mine, he kisses the inside of my leg and ever so slowly kisses up my thigh. I can feel the heat of his breath and I moan, he hasn't even kissed me where I want him and I'm already panting.

He kisses the top of my mound. "Mmmmmm, Flynn, please," I beg. I need more like I need my next breath.

"With pleasure," he growls before he licks from my taint to clit.

"Yes," I mewl, as he continues to devour me. The scruff on his face feels amazing, it heightens the pleasure coursing through me. Gripping his head in my hands, I press him farther into me. He attacks me with vigor and I'm loving every minute of it. He slips a finger inside and bends it, to hit that sweet spot that sets me off and suddenly, I'm screaming his name as I come all over his fingers and face.

He stands up to full height and gazes down at me. His face is covered in my juices, I lick my lips. Sitting up, I lean forward, grip his cheeks in my palms and press my lips to his. Since falling for Flynn, I've become a fan of kissing him after he goes down on me.

With my lips still pressed to his, I flip open his button, lower the fly, and push his jeans and briefs down his thighs. Wrapping my legs around his waist, I guide his cock toward my entrance and with a flick of his hips, he thrusts inside of me. Pistoning his hips back and forth, my body begins to tingle with orgasm number two.

"Let go," he murmurs against my lips.

It's all the prompting I need. I let the feelings envelop me and I crash over the edge for the second time tonight. Flynn soon follows, grunting through his release.

When he's finished, he rests his forehead against mine. We breathlessly stare at one another, completely sated and happy. He scoops me into his arms and walks us into the en suite bathroom, we shower and climb into bed together. Flynn lies on his back, and I snuggle into his side, throwing my leg over his. Looking up at the man who has become me world, I whisper, "I'm going to love living with you, Flynn Kelly."

"And I'm going to love living with you too, Avery Evans."

"All right, I'm off." She stops in front of me. "I'm so nervous."

"Why are you nervous?" Wrapping my arms around her waist, I gaze down into her sparkling green eyes.

"I'm scared I'll get there and they'll tell me it's an error and she's not coming home today."

"Bay is coming home today, tell that overactive imagination of yours to settle down."

"And you are one-hundred-perfect sure it's okay for her to stay here?"

"Of course, she's your sister. Will it suck to not be able to bend you over the island counter and fuck you when I want? Yes, but it's not forever. From what I know of your sister, she'll want her own place and independence before I get sick of her."

She smiles. "When did you get so wise?"

"I've always been wise, you're just noticing it now."

"Let me bow down to you then, ohh wise one." She steps back and bows down.

"Smart-ass." Looking at the clock, I tap her ass. "You better get going, otherwise, you'll be late."

"Okay, wish me luck."

"Good luck, not that you'll need it." *I'm the one who needs luck if I'm going to pull this off.* "Now go on, get, my other girlfriend is on her way over."

She playfully smack me in the chest. "Hardy, har-har." She kisses me on the lips and as she walks away, she looks over her shoulder. "Say hi to Ms. Palmer for me."

Shaking my head, I laugh and watch as my girlfriend, soon to be fiancée—I hope—exits the penthouse. When I hear the ding of the elevator, I race into my office and grab the fairy lights, candles, and flowers I stashed in here earlier, thankful she was in the shower when Max delivered it all. With my arms full, I head out to the patio to turn this place into a sparkly romantic wonderland.

Cress is onboard to get here around six with Lexi, who seems to be doing much better now. It was touch and go for a while after the accident, but with Preston on her case, and how he feels about Cress, it's good to see the little munchkin running around, happy and giggling again. Now, we just need Preston and Cress to pull their heads out of their asses and get their act together. Now that Lexi is healthy again, I think she will play a big part in that.

I've asked them to be here too, as I want all of Avery's 'family' here when I ask her the most important question of her, and my, life.

Time seems to be dragging by and finally my phone pings.

CRESS: *On our way up*

Cress had arranged with Avery to meet here when the sisters return, but little does Ave know that Cress was going to be here anyway. The ding of the elevator causes my heart rate to accelerate and rapidly race within in chest. The front door swings open and they all walk in.

"Hi, Bay," I say, as I wrap her in a hug.

"All set?" she whispers, and I nod my head.

A lump forms in the back of my throat and I feel like I want to throw up. I'm so fucking nervous. We stand in the foyer chatting when Avery says, "Come on in, no need to stand in the foyer all night." She looks vibrant and happy right now, and then her words register.

"No," I shout, startling everyone. "Ave lass, ummm, ahh, can I speak with you for a moment please... privately...outside."

She looks at me suspiciously but nods her head and starts walking outside. "Back in a sec." Cress and Bay both nod and grin like fools. Taking a deep breath, I follow behind her and when she steps outside, I flick the switch on the remote in my hand and the area lights up. Ave stops midstep, gasps, and covers her mouth.

Stepping around her, I take her hands in mine. She pulls her gaze to mine, her eyes sparkling and glassy with unshed tears. "Ave lass, I was falling for you from the moment I laid eyes on you at the Tavern. That first night was the best night of my life. The next morning you were gone and I was crushed, but fate had other ideas. We ran into each other again and this time, I didn't let you go. The more time I spent with you, the harder I fell. I knew you were the one for me, and I hope you feel the same way." Dropping to my knee, I pull the ring from my pocket. It's white gold with a round brilliant-cut diamond in a halo style. I place it at the tip of her ring finger. "Avery Evans, will you marry me?"

She's frozen and doesn't say anything for what feels like eternity. Then she nods her head and the biggest smile ever graces her face. "Yes. Yes. Yes. Flynn, yes, I'll marry you."

Sliding the ring on to her finger, she lifts her hand and gazes at it. Then her eyes land on mine. I have never been happier than I am in this moment. She grips my cheeks in her palms and covers my mouth with hers. Her tongue slides effortlessly into mine and our first kiss as an engaged couple is amazing.

The moment is interrupted when Cress, Preston, Lexi, and Baylor join us outside. The girls all have sparklers in their hands and smiles on their faces too.

"I'm engaged!" Ave joyously shouts.

The girls race over to her and admire her ring. Preston walks to me and we do the one-arm bro hug. "Congrats, dude."

"Thanks," I say, as I watch my fiancée with her friends. I fell hard for Avery Evans and each day I fall harder for her. I now get to spend the rest of my life with the most amazing woman in the world. I'm a lucky lucky man.

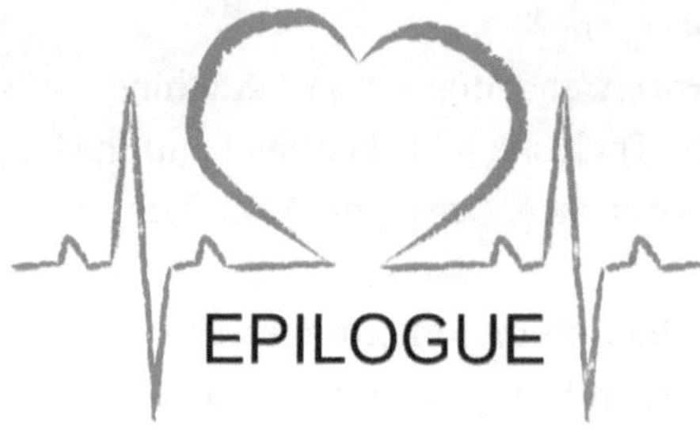

EPILOGUE

My life was plain and boring, and then one day I met Flynn Kelly and my world was turned upside and inside out. From the first moment I laid eyes on him, I started falling. We are complete opposites but as the saying goes 'opposites attract' and even though that's definitely the case with us, we go together perfectly.

I thought the day Flynn proposed was the happiest day of my life. And it was, until the day I became Mrs. Avery Kelly, but that moment has once again been trumped. Today, I gave birth to our twin boys, Marvin and Marshall. In honor of a great man who was taken too soon. His memory will live on in the form of these two little boys.

"How you doing?" Flynn asks, as he gazes down at our boys sleeping in their bassinet.

Standing up, I walk, well, shuffle, over to him and wrap my arm around his waist and look down at our munchkins. A smile graces my face. "Considering I just punched two watermelons out of my va-jay-jay, I'm pretty good. I think I'm still high though, everything is fuzzy, and I'm guessing I look like a hot mess."

"I'd say a sexy hot mess." Placing a kiss on my head, he hugs me closer to him.

"You need your eyes checked, I'm sure there's an optometrist around here somewhere."

"My eye sight is perfectly fine, Avery Kelly."

"Pffft, whatever you say." I pause. "We did good, didn't we?"

"Yep, they are perfect. Just like their momma."

"And just like their daddy. You think Marvin is up there gloating to everyone that we named them after him?"

"I have no doubt. And knowing the Houdini he is, I bet he's trying to find a way to get back down here so he can see them in the flesh."

I laugh and startle the boys. "Oops." I shrug. We each pick up a baby and like the pros we are—not—we rock them back to sleep….an hour and a half later. Who knew two, tiny, cute little beings could make so much noise? Once they are asleep again, we place them back in the bassinet and stare down at them.

Flynn pulls me into his side and kisses my head, before grabbing my hand and tugging me toward the bed. "We sleep when they sleep," he whispers, as we climb into the tiny hospital bed and snuggle.

"I love you, Flynn."

"I love you too, Ave."

He places a kiss on my forehead and I close my eyes.

As I drift off to sleep in Flynn's arms, I realize I'm the luckiest girl alive. Falling for Dr. Kelly was the best decision I ever made; not that I stood a chance when it came to my sexy as sin Irish stud.

THE END!

To find out what happens with Lexi, Preston and Cress,
pre-order Falling for Dr. Knight now.
Their story is coming 3 June 2020

Chaos and tragedy can either bring us together, or tear us apart.
Falling in love isn't like it is in fairy tales.

CRESSIDA

Being a single mom is hard.
But Lexi is my life, and I'll do anything for my daughter.
I just never expected tragedy to strike, or for my past to haunt us.
Or for Dr. Preston Knight to be the man who saves us.
The same man I should *never* have fallen in love with.

PRESTON

I'm the best in my field.
Being a doctor is in my *blood*.
My focus is always on my career.
Until her—Cressida Bayliss.
I've fought many battles, but never one so close to my heart.
This is the biggest fight of my life, and with my heart on the line, I can't afford to lose.

She's the twin you love to hate. Will Baylor get her HEA and redeem herself?
Find out late 2020, preorder Falling for Agent Cox today.

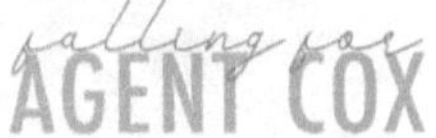

There's a fine line between love and hate.
A love fueled from hate is the strongest of them all.

BAYLOR
My life hasn't gone as I planned, but it's all my doing.
I'm given a second chance.
But I didn't count on him—Agent Corey Cox.
He's on the straight and narrow, abiding by the rules.
He calms my inner beast and makes me want to be a better person.
When my past reappears, that wildness inside sparks to life again.
Is his love enough to stop me turning my back on everything I've worked so hard for?

COREY
I live my life by the book.
Being an agent is everything to me.
The lines are never blurred.
Until her—Baylor Evans.
She's wild, carefree, and marches to the beat of her own drum.
She brings out a side to me I never knew existed.

But it all implodes, when I'm faced with an impossible decision.
Either way I lose.

PLAYLIST

Can't Help Falling in Love – Elvis Presley
Unchained Melody – the Righteous Brothers
Can't Take my Eyes off You – Engelbert Humphries
Sexy Back – Justin Timberlake
Bleeding Love – Leona Lewis
Love Song – Sara Bareilles
Complicated – Avril Lavigne
I Don't Wanna Be – Gavin DeGraw
Acceptable in the 80's – Calvin Harris
Pony – Genuwine
Wolves – Selena Gomez
Havana – Camila Cabello
Way Down We Go – KALEO
A Thousand Miles – Vanessa Carlton
Big Girls Don't Cry – Fergie
Hey, Soul Sister – Train
Walkin' on the Sun – Smash Mouth
Escape (The Pina Colada Song) – Rupert Holmes
American Woman – Lenny Kravitz
You've Lost That Lovin Feelin' – The Righteous Brothers
Hey There Delilah – Plain White T's
Better in Time - Leona Lewis
Halo – Beyonce
Just The Way You Are – Bruno Mars
Not N Cold – Katy Perry
How to Save a Life – The Fray
Who Knew – P!nk
Toxic – Brittney Spears
Chasing Cars – Snow Patrol
Haven't Met You Yet – Michael Buble

Just Dance – Lady Gaga
Dynamite – Taio Cruz
Crazy in Love – Beyonce & Jay-Z
Bring me to Life – Evanescence
I Can't Go for That (No can do) – Hall & Oates
Kiss on my List - Hall & Oates
Out of Touch - Hall & Oates
Private Eyes - Hall & Oates
Maneater - Hall & Oates
Mr. Brightside – The Killers
Never Tear us Apart – INXS
Lover – Taylor Swift
All of Me – John Legend

This playlist can be found on spotify.

ACKNOWLEDGEMENTS

To, **my family; Troy, Piper** and **Kade.** You three are my rocks, my loveable pains in the butt. You are my everything. Love you all to the moon and back XoXoX

My beta babes; **Alley, Andi, Cherie, Halle, Jenny** and **Trisha;** thank you ladies once again for reading my book baby and giving me your opinions and feedback. You gals are rock stars and I would be lost without you.
Special shout out to **Alley, Halle** and **Jenny** for pushing me to make Dr. Kelly a full length novel.

My editor, **Karen**, from **Barren Acres Editing;** I'm running out of things to say. You're not only my editor, but you're also a great friend; why do you live so far away? Thank you, once again for helping me turn my book baby from a pile of crap into a beautiful book baby.

My cover designer, **Kristie** from **Vanilla Lily Designs**. As soon as I saw this cover, I knew it was Avery and Flynn.

With the little tweeks I asked for, you made it absolutely perfect. Thank you for a gorgeous cover.

To the following authors; **Chloe Renee, Corinne Mazille, Renee Linda, Tara Lee, Alley Ciz, Cass Fowler, Linda Higgins** and **SE Roberts;** thank you for your support, encouragement and writing sprints. Without you guys, I'd be a mess in the corner drinking wine from my coffee mug.

To **my readers**, thank you for the kind words that you message me with each release. 9 out of 10 times, these arrive just when I need a pick me up and they always do. From the bottom of my heart, thank you for supporting me and my books.

Cheers,
Dana Xo

FACEBOOK ~ INSTAGRAM ~ BOOKBUB

GOODREADS ~ WEBSITE

dlgallieauthor@outlook.com

Sign up to my newsletter

ABOUT THE AUTHOR

DL Gallie is from Queensland, Australia, but she's lived in many different places all over the world, including the UK and Canada. She currently resides in Central Queensland with her husband and two munchkins. She and her husband have been together since she was sixteen, and although they drive each other crazy at times, she couldn't imagine her life without him.

Shortly after her son was born, DL began reading again. With encouragement from her husband, she picked up the pen and started writing, and now the voices in her head won't shut up.

DL enjoys listening to music, drinking white wine in the summer, red wine in the winter, and beer all year round. She's also never been known to turn down a cocktail, especially a margarita.

www.ingramcontent.com/pod-product-compliance
Lightning Source LLC
Chambersburg PA
CBHW020126120726
47903CB00007B/2125